THE WEDDING AT WILLOW HEIGHTS

WILLOW HEIGHTS SERIES BOOK FIVE

ABIGAIL BECK

CHAPTER 1

ary Elle and Thomas walked hand in hand to the main office at Willow Acres. She took a deep breath as a soft gust of wind blew by. She was enjoying living in the mountains. Every night after dinner, she and Thomas usually sat outside discussing their day while sipping on a warm cup of tea and enjoying all the smells and nature sounds.

Thomas loved hearing about her day and any new ideas she came up with. He was always encouraging and selfless. Any time Mary Elle decided she wanted to pursue something, Thomas found a way of making it possible. What she most loved about Thomas was that he cared. He cared about all those around him. He was the person you could call at any time of day, and you knew he would be there to help. With his birthday coming up in a couple of months, she wanted to show him how much she and everyone else cared about him. It was time he realized just how much he meant to each of them.

As Mary Elle glanced over at Thomas, she thanked God for bringing him into her life. She was still in disbelief that this was her life now. It hadn't been long since she'd been in an unhappy marriage where she was often alone in a big, empty house. Now, she had her two daughters close by and was married to a man that showed her daily what it was like to be in a genuine loving relationship.

If only she could get her son, Michael, to move nearby, she understood that his life and plans were different. He had a distinguished career and life in California. He was newly engaged, and although Mary Elle was still not too fond of his fiancée, she didn't step in. She trusted her kids to make their own choices in life, and above all, she trusted God would lead them and protect them.

"Penny for your thoughts?" Thomas asked her as he gave her a small nudge. This was a typical exchange for them. Mary Elle was often in her head planning different things or thinking about her kids and life in general.

"Not much. Just the usual," she said.

"And what's the usual?" Thomas asked with that smile of his that still made her heart skip.

"You, the kids, and this wonderful place we call home."

"This place became a home the moment you moved in," Thomas said as he put an arm around her shoulders, "I don't know what I would've done if you hadn't come into my life."

Mary Elle felt a blush creeping in. How had she gotten so lucky with this man?

"I'm very happy God brought you into my life, too."

They came to a stop when they spotted Jasper by the stables.

"Any luck yet?" Thomas asked Jasper, the farmhand.

"Not yet, but I feel it will be any day now," Jasper said as he wiped the sweat from his brow.

One of their highlander cows was pregnant and was due any day now. They'd been anxiously awaiting the baby calf.

"How are things going around here? Do you need any help?" Thomas asked as he joined Jasper at the stables.

"Not for now, but I might need help in the future," Mary Elle heard Jasper say as she went off to the office. Thomas stayed behind, catching up with Jasper.

"Good morning, ladies," Mary Elle said when she spotted Molly and Bailey at the front desk.

"Good morning!" they both called out.

"Is anything going on?" she asked them.

"We have the new part-time receptionist coming in soon," Molly said.

"That's right! I'd forgotten about that. How's your first week of classes going?"

Molly was going back to school after taking a year off. Molly was the eldest of her siblings and got the job at Willow Acres to help her mother with their house bills. Her mother looked after her elderly father and worked two jobs. Molly would continue operating the front desk at Willow Acres part-time and pick up shifts at the restaurant on the weekends.

"They're good. I am enjoying being back in school," Molly said, smiling brightly.

"That's great to hear. I'm sure you'll make us all proud."

Mary Elle finished clocking in and headed to her office, where she began reading her work emails.

"Mary Elle?"

"Yes?" Mary Elle said as she glanced up from her computer and found Molly standing at her door. Molly stepped into the office and closed the door quietly behind her.

"Lorraine called this morning asking for you. She says it's urgent you call her back," Molly said as she placed a message memo on her desk.

"Lorraine?" Mary Elle asked, confused.

She felt all the color drain from her face. Lorraine had abandoned Wyatt when she ran off with a new boyfriend. Wyatt had been left with no food, water, or electricity. A teacher had filed a report, and he went to live with his grandmother for a short time. His mother never showed up at court, which resulted in Mary Elle and Thomas adopting the young boy.

"Yes, Wyatt's mom."

"Did she say what she wanted? Is she back in town?" Mary Elle asked as she quickly grabbed her phone. She had to tell Thomas.

"No, she only said to tell you she called. She said not to mention anything to Wyatt."

"Did you say anything to him?" Mary Elle asked, concerned.

She wasn't sure how Wyatt would react. Things for him hadn't been easy since his mother left. He was being bullied at school, and he was dealing with all kinds of emotions that were bringing him down. Mary Elle couldn't even imagine what he was going through or how this news might affect him.

"No, of course not."

"Okay. Please don't. I don't know how he will take this. I'll speak to her to see what is going on, and then we'll decide what to say to him."

"Okay," Molly said as she awkwardly stood there before turning around.

Molly and Wyatt had started dating recently. Mary Elle and Thomas had been caught by surprise when Mary Elle walked in on them in his bedroom. They'd since then set ground rules, and the young couple was doing a great job of staying in line. Mary Elle knew Molly had a soft spot for Wyatt and could be trusted with this information.

* * *

"I THINK you're going to love this one," Charlotte, the sales associate at the wedding dress shop in Winding Creek, said as she brought a new dress out.

Melanie, Mary Elle, Tiffany, DeeAnn, and Rita spent the day bridal dress shopping. Melanie was over the moon planning her wedding. She still couldn't believe that she was getting a second chance at love. She loved Cade so much. He made her happy and taught her how to love and forgive herself, but most importantly, he loved Ryder. She couldn't wait for Ryder to have siblings and see their little family grow. There was no doubt in her mind that God had brought him into her life.

"I hope I'm not late!" Brittney said as she walked into the boutique.

Her hair was down, and her natural highlights shined in the sun. Brittney was a ray of light everywhere she went. She always had a smile on her face, and she let no one go by unacknowledged. Melanie met her while she lived in New York, and they'd become the best of friends in no time. Brittney wrote a travel column for the women's magazine Melanie worked as the creative director.

"I'm so glad you could make it!" Melanie said as she rushed over to her friend.

"I wouldn't miss it. I plan on staying here until your wedding day. You're not getting rid of me!" Brittney said as the two friends laughed and hugged.

"I'm honored. The globetrotting influencer is staying in Willow Heights, just for me." Melanie said with a wink.

Apart from writing the weekly column for the magazine, Brittney was an influencer and traveled all over the world. She had amassed millions of followers that relied on her for reviews on the best places to visit, eat, or stay. Shortly after

Mary Elle moved to Willow Heights, the girls had visited, and Brittney wrote a review for Willow Acres. After her review, Willow Acres had gotten lots of new visitors. The town had also benefitted from all the new travelers. Other influencers had visited as well, and now the town was bustling with new businesses.

"It's great to have you back in town," Mary Elle said as Brittney joined them in the sitting area, waiting to see the next dress Melanie would model for them.

"I'm excited to be back in Willow Heights. Melanie told me that Main Square has new restaurants and shops. Mrs. Adelman invited me to stay at her inn, and I can't wait to review it and bring her lots of new guests."

"That's amazing, Brittney. We all know how great things turned out with your last review and helped with getting new clients," Mary Elle said as Melanie walked out in front of them.

Melanie was beautiful and beaming. Her happiness was evident, and she looked amazing in this gown, but was it the one?

"Mel, you look gorgeous," Tiffany said as happy tears began welling in her eyes.

"Stop it, don't cry," Melanie said, holding back all her emotions. She fanned her face to keep the tears at bay.

"Is this the one?" Mary Elle asked as she came to stand next to Melanie.

They stared at her reflection in the mirror. Melanie had never felt more beautiful than she did now.

"Yes, I love this dress," Melanie said as she gave a small twirl.

"Is there any other dress you might want to try, or are you completely sure this is the one?" Charlotte asked.

"I guess I'll try the dress that Rita picked out," Melanie replied as she gave Rita's hand a small squeeze.

Melanie loved Rita as an aunt. Rita had always been there for them. She was Mary Elle's best friend, and they always spent holidays, birthdays, and vacations together.

"Melanie will be an amazing wife to Cade. I love seeing how they treat each other, and the love Cade has for little Ryder is undeniable. God truly blessed them by bringing them together," Rita said as she, too, wiped happy tears from her face.

This was such an emotional shopping trip that few people understood how unhappy and unhealthy Melanie's first marriage had been. She had been a devoted wife that just wanted to please her husband and raise a family, but Everett did not share the same feelings or ideas as Melanie. This caused many issues in their marriage, which ultimately ended in divorce when Everett found out Melanie was pregnant with his child.

Everett did not want to be a part of the baby's life or continue his marriage with Melanie. He did not wish to have a family of his own. He was an only child and was highly ambitious and a workaholic. Being a father wasn't something he ever wanted. Melanie suffered a lot of verbal and emotional abuse while they were together. Their relationship had been very toxic. Melanie had prayed God would bless her with a child, and God answered her prayer with little Ryder. Now, God had blessed her with Cade. He was the complete opposite of Everett, and their relationship couldn't be compared. Melanie was convinced that God did everything in His perfect timing and that His will is always good for those that love him.

"Well, here is Rita's choice," Melanie said as she appeared once again before them.

"Melanie, you make all these dresses look amazing. How do you like this one?" Rita asked.

"I like this dress. It's elegant and beautiful, but this isn't the one for me." Melanie said as Rita walked toward her to hug her.

"Thanks for trying it on for me," Rita said as she hugged Melanie.

"I guess we found the one. How about the shoes and veil?" Mary Elle asked Melanie.

"I got the shoes; I just need the veil," Melanie said as she gestured for Charlotte to help her with the veil selection.

Melanie would wear her favorite heels. She'd bought them at a sample sale in New York and had never worn them. They were designer and had been pretty pricey even at sample sale prices, but she couldn't leave them behind. She knew from the moment she saw them; that they were special. They had a stiletto heel and straps adorned with pearls and Swarovski crystals, and they had the red bottoms that were a signature of the brand.

The bridal dress shopping trip had taken all day. Melanie rushed home, where Cade was babysitting Ryder. Tiffany and Brittney drove to the Inn together, and DeeAnn went on a date with Paul. Rita and Mary Elle went out for coffee before heading back to their houses.

"How's the jewelry making going?" Mary Elle asked Rita, who had just ordered a cappuccino with a blueberry muffin.

"Great. Sienna and I are bonding a lot. She helps me whenever she's in town, and we are just having a blast. How's Wyatt doing?" Rita asked, concerned that Lorraine had called Mary Elle.

"Well, I called her, and she said she was in town for a little, but she wasn't staying. She asked about Wyatt, and I told her they had bullied him at school. I also told her he has a girlfriend." Mary Elle said as she took a sip of her French vanilla latte.

"At least she checked in on him."

Mary Elle knew she should be grateful that Lorraine had

checked in on Wyatt. She knew from Rita's experience that her sister Emma had never once tried to contact her or the kids. It was a mystery what had happened to Emma, and they had all long-lost hope of ever seeing her again.

"You're right; I'm not sure if this will affect Wyatt. He already has a lot going on. I don't want to stir up the past or past emotions that might have already started healing. He's going to play basketball next season. I think that will help him ease his mind as well."

"Sports always help. I know with Alexander and Andrew, it helped them keep busy and focused. Mandy did better with art and music. If sports don't work with Wyatt, try art and music," Rita said confidently.

"Good to know. I know Wyatt likes basketball. I know he will do great once he gets comfortable with the team, and I hope that will help him build his confidence and self-esteem." Mary Elle said as she finished her latte.

Soon it was time to head back home. Mary Elle and Rita said their goodbyes and planned to meet again to review some inventory Rita had set aside for Mary Elle. Rita had also been working secretly on a beautiful, unique piece for Melanie. It had pearls and sapphires. It would be her "something blue" for the wedding.

CHAPTER 2

iffany and Mrs. Adelman stood at the front desk counter checking a couple in when David walked into the Inn. Tiffany felt her heart quicken at the sight of him. A month had already passed since she'd proclaimed her feelings for him in front of everyone at Melanie and Cade's engagement dinner. David came by the Inn every morning and had breakfast with her in the kitchen. She loved starting her day with him. When the couple went off with Mrs. Adelman as she showed them to their room, David approached Tiffany.

"Good morning, beautiful," he said as he gave her a light kiss.

Tiffany ducked her head to hide her blush as they pulled apart. She wasn't used to having a boyfriend or public displays of affection. Mrs. Adelman cleared her throat to announce her return.

"Good morning, Mrs. Adelman," David said as he bent down to kiss her on the cheek.

"Good morning, my sweet boy," she said as she patted his cheek.

"I wanted to fix the leak at the kitchen sink while I'm here," he told her.

"Don't worry about that. That's what I keep Mr. Behr on call for."

"I have your delicious breakfast with your gorgeous employee and fix the kitchen sink for you. It's an even exchange. No need to bother Mr. Behr."

"Well, if you insist. I know there's no way of swaying a Clarke man when he's got his mind set up."

David gave her a wink and grabbed his tool bag before heading into the kitchen.

"He's such a good guy," Mrs. Adelman mused once he was out of earshot.

"He is," Tiffany said with a smile.

"How are things going between you two?"

"They're good. He's so sweet and patient. I'm new to all this, and I don't know if he wanted someone more experienced. Someone more expressive."

"Don't overthink things, sweetie. He seems happy, and so do you."

"But overthinking is my specialty," Tiffany said with a small laugh.

Tiffany knew Mrs. Adelman was right. She should enjoy her relationship with David and live in the moment, but she often stayed up at night wondering if he was truly happy with her. Tiffany wasn't like other girls; she had been a late bloomer. She had always kept to herself and been too focused on the goals she set for herself that she'd never had an actual boyfriend until now. That had always been an insecurity for her, but it was something she was working on currently. She wanted to be the best person she could be for herself and David.

"Good morning, ladies," Mr. Gunner said as he appeared with a crate of milk jugs.

He delivered fresh milk daily from his farm, but unlike before, he now stuck around to have breakfast with Mrs. Adelman. Now that Mrs. Adelman wasn't avoiding him, that is. He kissed Mrs. Adelman on the cheek, which made Tiffany smile. She loved seeing them together, and she was so happy that they were getting a second chance at love. In her short time in Willow Heights, Mrs. Adelman had become not only Tiffany's boss but also one of her dearest friends. It hadn't been long since they were single and look at them now, in loving relationships with the men of their dreams.

"Where's David?" Mr. Gunner asked.

"He's fixing the leak in the kitchen. Why don't you help him? Tiffany and I will be right in with breakfast," Mrs. Adelman said.

The couples now sat together around the kitchen island, enjoying their breakfast. They preferred eating here than in the dining room with the guests. Mrs. Adelman had always given the guests privacy during their meals but joined them for dinner now and then.

"Whenever you two are free, I would love to show you the Animal Sanctuary," David told them.

"I wondered when you would invite us," Mrs. Adelman said.

"That might be dangerous. I have a feeling she'll return home with a pet or two," Mr. Gunner said as he looked lovingly at Mrs. Adelman.

"I have a couple of goats, a few turkeys, and a rooster with a broken leg. I found him on the side of the road yesterday. All the dogs and kittens have found new homes."

"Who says she won't bring home a goat?" Mr. Gunner said with a laugh.

"They are adorable. Many people have them as pets," Tiffany said as she winked at Mrs. Adelman.

"That's true. The Inn needs a pet," Mrs. Adelman said with a sly smile.

"Maybe we don't make any rash decisions, eh?" Mr. Gunner said as he pulled her close and kissed her cheek.

* * *

MELANIE AND BRITTNEY were having lunch at Willow Acres when Lisa and Patty joined them.

"What do you all suggest I try?" Brittney asked as she picked up her menu.

"Everything Dean makes is great, so you can't go wrong with anything," Patty said with a proud smile.

"Normally, I would say that the chef's girlfriend is biased, but I agree with Patty. Dean knows his way around the kitchen." Lisa said as she took a sip of her water.

"My favorite is his cranberry chicken salad for lunch. It's light but filling," Melanie said as she sent Mary Elle a quick text to check on Ryder. Mary Elle was working through lunch, and Melanie had left him sleeping in his playpen. A door connected Mary Elle's and Melanie's offices, which she'd left open so her mom could hear him in case he woke from his nap.

"So, what's the hot cowboy's story?" Brittney asked with a mischievous look on her face.

"Cowboy?" they all asked in confusion.

Melanie followed Brittney's gaze and noticed Jasper walking by. He was wearing jeans, a button-down shirt, and boots. He was even wearing a belt with a large buckle and a hat. She never noticed how much he looked like a cowboy until now.

"That's Jasper. He's great, but he keeps to himself," Lisa told her.

"Yeah, he's a bit of a mystery. I've never seen him with any girlfriends or boyfriends, for that matter," Patty said with a shrug.

"He's straight. He dated Michelle for a few years, but he hasn't dated since. Are you interested? I can introduce you." Lisa asked as she wiggled her brows.

"I'm not sticking around here for very long, but he is very nice to look at."

"Why don't you get to know him while you are here? It never hurts to make new cute friends." Melanie said with a feeling that maybe Jasper would enjoy Brittney's friendship.

"Everyone needs friends, especially handsome ones," Lisa agreed.

"I'm starving. I guess I'll try Dean's bourbon cheeseburger with fries." Melanie said as she sat her menu down.

Dean was constantly updating the menu and changing things up. He always kept the most requested dishes on the menu for his regulars.

"The zucchini fries are delicious too," Patty added as she looked over the menu.

"It must be nice to have a man that cooks this well," Lisa said as she gave Patty a light nudge.

"It is a blessing. He's amazing all around, though." Patty said, giggling.

"I think I'll go visit the animals in the barn after lunch," Brittney said as she looked to where Jasper was sitting, waiting for his lunch.

"Why wait until after lunch?" Melanie asked as she suddenly called out to Jasper and waved him over. Jasper came to their table and greeted everyone.

"Hello, ladies," he said, smiling as he glanced around the table.

"Why don't you join us for lunch?" Melanie asked Jasper.

"I would love to, but I'm waiting for an on-the-go lunch I

just ordered. I'm leaving work early to help David with a side project," Jasper said.

"Maybe next time. Oh! I almost forgot. Brittney mentioned that she wanted to stop by the barn to spend some time with the animals and maybe get a horseback ride. Maybe she can stop by tomorrow?" Melanie asked, taking advantage of this moment to make some progress between the two.

Jasper was a fantastic guy, and her best friend deserved someone like him. Melanie was usually not fond of the guys Brittney dated. She found it weird that Brittney often talked about falling in love and all that jazz but always picked guys that were so far off from what she described as her dream man. Maybe it was because of her lifestyle or the people she was surrounded by.

"That would be great. Brittney, you can stop by whenever you would like," Jasper said as the server called out his name and handed him his lunch.

"See you tomorrow!" Brittney called out after him.

Jasper turned back and waved at them.

He was a good guy, like most guys from Willow Heights. Jasper was a gentleman and had great manners. That type of man is hard to find in the city. Men in the city rarely treated women with chivalry. Melanie remembered riding the subway in NYC and standing the entire ride because men her age and younger wouldn't give her their seat. Another time she was walking out of work with her arms full of files, and the guy in front of her didn't hold the door open, and it slammed into her, causing all her files to fall all over the place. He didn't even apologize and just went on his way.

"It seems like the wedding date is creeping up so fast! You must be so excited, Mel." Patty said, bringing Melanie's attention back to the table.

"Oh, yes. I can't wait! I finally found my dress, and I can't wait for Cade to see me in it," Melanie answered.

"You are beaming. I can feel your happiness radiating from you," Lisa said as she dipped a piece of bread in oil.

"Did you girls receive your invitations? I know the mail around here can be a little slow. I should've just handed them to you myself."

"I got mine, and I am so excited about your bridal shower," Brittney said with an evil laugh.

"I forgot to tell you; we want to combine the bridal shower with the bachelor's party. Mom and Thomas are coordinating. You know I couldn't say no to mom. Plus, I think it will be fun to party together with the guys." Melanie explained and hoped they would like the idea.

"Sounds fun, as long as we party! Woo hoo!" Patty exclaimed.

CHAPTER 3

Mary Elle was in the kitchen when Thomas walked in. She was making his favorite herb-crusted salmon with roasted lemons. They had both been running around all week and hadn't had a moment to catch up. Mary Elle wrapped things up a little earlier to have dinner ready for him. She'd brought Ryder along since Melanie had a few wedding details to take care of. Thomas walked in and gave her a light kiss before asking her about her week.

"It was interesting. I spoke with Lorraine the other day. She wanted to check on Wyatt. She wanted to know if he's ok and how he was adjusting to living with us," she told him. Mary Elle meant to tell Thomas the day it happened, but she hadn't been able to get a moment alone with him until now.

"Are you going to tell him you spoke with her?" Thomas asked as he served himself a glass of water and took a seat on the kitchen island.

"I'm not sure. I don't want to affect his progress. He's been adjusting well until the whole bullying issue came along. I also spoke with Rita, and she suggested we get him

17

involved in sports or art and music. She said it helped her with the kids."

"That's a great idea. He likes basketball. I know we had talked about it before. He's been working the weekends to make money, but I'll speak with him and work out something with his allowance. He's a hardworking kid."

Before the adoption, Wyatt worked more hours at Willow Acres, but to get his grades up, Thomas and Mary Elle had opted only to have him work on the weekends. Before the adoption, he had worked during the week after school. He was in a school work program and had days where he was only in school for half the day. Once he got his grades back up, he would return to his old schedule at Willow Acres.

"I know. He's a great kid. He deserves so much more in life, and I want him to be happy," Mary Elle said as she checked on the food.

"I know, honey. I do too. He's our boy now. We can help him and guide him. I'll talk to him. Don't worry," Thomas said as he stretched his back.

"Thanks, darling. You are an incredible role model, and I know he looks up to you and loves you dearly. How was your day? I didn't' see you at all today."

"It was busy. I met with the town council for a list of repairs they want to be done at the Inn. I don't want to have Mrs. Adelman's problems with them. I still think all of this is bogus and just their way of intimidating her into selling the inn."

"I agree. Are there a lot of repairs to be made?"

"There are a few things, but nothing that we can't handle," Thomas said, giving her a reassuring smile.

Mary Elle grabbed Ryder from his playpen and joined Thomas on the kitchen island. Thomas pulled out his cellphone and took a picture of her before she could protest.

"What was that?" she asked, surprised by his action.

"I like this, you and me, and a little child. We should have shared this. I wish we could've had kids together and raised a family."

Mary Elle felt her heart flutter. She had always wondered what it would have been like to have married Thomas instead of Bill all those years ago. She wondered what it might have been like to raise a family with him instead. However, she knew she wouldn't have her kids if things had worked out that way.

"Me too. You would've been a wonderful father. No, I take that back. You are a wonderful father to Wyatt. He is so blessed to have you."

There was a light knock on the kitchen side door before Melanie walked in.

"I've missed you so much today!" Melanie said as she took Ryder from Mary Elle and snuggled him close.

Ryder loved Melanie and always gave her the biggest and best smile. He was like Mary Elle and loved to give people hugs, and even at his young age, he grabbed on tight. Ryder was a joy to have around. He was a happy-go-lucky little guy.

"Hey Melanie, you came early for him," Mary Elle said.

"Yeah, my meeting was shorter than I thought. That Bride sure is a Bridezilla," Melanie said with an exaggerated roll of her eyes and a laugh.

"Oh Mel, you are a Bridezilla, alright. So did you find the flower shop in Winding Creek?" Mary Elle asked, realizing Melanie was referring to herself as being a Bridezilla.

"If there's any time to act crazy and get away with it, it's while planning your wedding," Thomas said with a wink before excusing himself.

"He's right." Mary Elle said as she poured Melanie a glass of lemonade.

"You'll never guess who else I saw while in Winding Creek?"

"Who?"

"Clarice seems like she's friends with the flower shop owner."

"I hope she doesn't cause trouble for you and Debbie. She has the best range of sunflowers in the area. After Willow Acres, of course," Mary Elle said, worried that Clarice would somehow put in a bad word for Melanie.

Melanie and Cade wanted to have a short engagement. Other couples had already booked Willow Acres in advance, so she had to use other vendors.

"After Clarice left, Debbie was fine with me. I gave her a deposit for the flowers, and we went over the centerpieces and bouquet. I don't think Clarice has done damage."

"I hope you are right."

"How did Ryder behave?" Melanie asked Mary Elle as she kissed Ryder on the top of his head.

"He's an angel, Mel. Ryder is a joy to be around. He's been laughing and smiling all day. He ate, slept, and played."

"Aw, he's such a good boy," Melanie said as she gave him another kiss.

"Has Cade mentioned anything about his planning with Thomas? I don't want to grill Thomas about details, but I'm sure we will handle the food and décor," Mary Elle said as she hinted at the guy's lack of attention to detail.

"I know. They want to barbecue our food. I heard them on the phone. I was like no! inside my head."

"Well, no, we want to have a nice meal!" Mary Elle said as they both laughed and planned on how to tell them they would not be barbecuing their food for the party.

"Let's get to planning this party already!" Melanie said excitedly.

"You don't need to worry about much of the planning. Rita, Sienna, and Tiffany are helping with the party. Please don't worry. It's your bridal shower, and I want you to enjoy it. Take time for yourself to sit back and take it all in."

"Thanks, mom. This is my first actual wedding. Everett and I just eloped and missed out on all of this. In hindsight, I guess it was meant to be that way. Now, with Cade, I can have my actual dream wedding. I never thought it would be this meaningful to plan it with so much love and detail and not rush into anything."

"You are so right, Melanie. This was the way it was meant to be. You won't take this experience for granted because you know what it was like to elope and miss out on the entire experience."

"I can't thank you enough for all you and the girls are doing for me. This means so much to me."

"Mel, you know I love planning and throwing in surprises. We do it all with love. Have you picked your bridesmaids?"

"Yes, Tiffany, Sienna, Brittney, and Ruby," Melanie said as she showed Mary Elle the special card and gift she made for them to ask them to be her bridesmaids.

"What about Amanda?" Mary Elle asked.

"I asked her, but she said she wouldn't be able to make it. She's going overseas for an internship soon. I think she's going to Germany."

"Oh, that's nice. Rita hasn't mentioned anything to me yet. I'm sure she'll tell me all about it."

"She just found out she got accepted, and they approved her visa paperwork. I'm sure Rita will tell you soon."

"Has Cade picked out his groomsmen?"

"Yes, he has, and he wanted to ask Michael but felt weird about it since they have never really spent time together, just casual gatherings."

"He has a point. Michael is coming with his fiancée, Samantha. I'm still not sure what to make of that relationship, but I'm willing to get to know her more. I want Michael to settle down instead of dating so much."

"Mom, pray that God brings him the right person. I'm sure God will answer your prayers and send him an exceptional woman to have a serious relationship with."

"You're right. I know God will answer my prayers and lead Michael down the right path."

* * *

"Hey stranger," Tiffany said as she walked into the barn where David checked the rooster's leg.

"Hey beautiful, how are you?" David asked as he turned to face her.

"I'm great now that I'm here," Tiffany said as she walked over to David and gave him a peck on his cheek.

"It's not nice to be all lovey-dovey in front of single people!" Brittney said with a laugh as she walked into the barn after Tiffany.

Tiffany had brought her along to show her the animal sanctuary and introduce her to its current residents.

"Welcome back to Willow Heights, Brittney," David said with a smile.

"Hey girls," Jasper said as he walked into the barn with an ointment and what seemed like a splint for the rooster.

"Hey there, I didn't know you were here. How are you, Jasper?" Tiffany asked.

"I'm doing good. Helping David with Mr. Rooster."

Brittney walked over to the rooster and noticed his broken leg. "Oh no, what happened to him?"

"I'm not sure. I found him on the side of the road with a broken leg. How is his leg, in your opinion?" David asked Jasper.

Jasper had lots of experience working and helping barn

animals. He worked as a veterinary technician before working at Willow Acres.

"Well, it seems like he got his leg run over or something. We can do a splint on him and see how it heals. If it doesn't heal, we might need to amputate his little leg to give him a more comfortable and painless life."

"Wow, that's serious," Tiffany said in a somber tone.

"Yeah, that's what Lindsay said this morning when I told her about Mr. Rooster," David said, agreeing with Jasper's take on the situation.

"Let's pray it doesn't come to amputation," Tiffany said as she gave David a weary look.

"I think Mr. Rooster is a champ. He's going to be alright," Jasper said as he ran a hand down the rooster's back.

Tiffany gave Brittney a tour of the animal sanctuary while the men cleaned up and fed the animals.

"Are you girls hungry?" David asked once they rejoined them.

"I'm starving," Tiffany said, as her stomach grumbled in agreement.

"I can never say no to food. What are you guys thinking?" Brittney asked them.

"There's a new gastropub over in Winding Creek we can check out," Jasper said.

"I've been meaning to take Tiffany there. I've heard great things about it. Let me close up, and we can head out," David told them.

CHAPTER 4

Brittney wasn't used to sitting around and doing nothing all day. She came to Willow Heights to help Melanie with her wedding. But she has also been tasked with a special assignment at work. So far, she had made little progress on that front. She came into Willow Acres with Melanie today, hoping to get some work done and make progress on that assignment. She scrolled through her emails and felt her stomach drop when she saw her boss asking for an update.

The magazine sent her to Willow Heights to convince Melanie to have her wedding featured in the magazine. Brittney knew how private her best friend was, and she wasn't sure how she would feel about having her wedding broadcasted. Brittney wasn't one to drag her feet on any of her work assignments, but she was afraid of putting a strain on their friendship. She took a deep breath and took a moment to stretch her back. They had returned late the night before from Winding Creek. The food and the ambiance were great at the gastropub. It had surprised her that such a small town would have a place like that.

The more time she spent in the area, the more she found the little town charming. Willow Heights had stolen a piece of her heart from the first time she visited. Everyone was so welcoming and kind. They had a way of making you feel at home. She loved going on walks around here without fear of being mugged or hit by a car. It was peaceful and beautiful, but she could never settle down in a place like this. She wanted to see the world, and there were still so many places she needed to visit and foods she needed to try.

Brittney let out a small groan when another email came in asking about the wedding. She wasn't ready to reply to that email yet. Brittney would wait until after lunch. She would ask Melanie then and get it over with. If she said no, the magazine would accept it, right?

"Hey, did you hear me?" a voice said, interrupting her thoughts.

"Jasper, hey! Sorry, I was lost in thought."

"Is everything okay?" he asked as he slid into the seat across from her.

Brittney worked at one of the restaurant's outside tables by the lake.

She couldn't help but notice how his green eyes seemed lighter today. Maybe it was the sun or that nice blue button-down shirt he was wearing with the sleeves rolled up to his elbows. He was a different kind of handsome. Not like the boys she usually dated back in New York. He was rough and manly. He didn't have an ounce of hair gel in his hair or perfectly groomed eyebrows.

"Yeah, everything is great. I feel a little useless being here and helping Mel with her wedding when I know nothing of the area. It would be much easier if she were getting married in New York," she said as she tried to rein in her thoughts. What had all that been about? Why did she find Jasper so intriguing?

"Sorry, I can't help you there."

"No experience planning extravagant weddings?" She asked with a raised brow.

"Nope, been very careful to steer clear of all that."

"Why? Don't you want the happy ever after? The kids? The picket fences?"

"It's hard to date when you live in a small town. It's been years since I went on a date."

"Have you tried dating apps?"

"No, thanks."

Britney couldn't believe what she was hearing. Everyone she knew was on dating apps. Sure, she didn't know anyone that married anyone they met on there, but that didn't mean it couldn't happen.

"You should! I can help you. It's all about your photo and how you present yourself."

"I can imagine you have no problem getting dates. Why do you use dating apps?" Jasper asked as he leaned in. His interest surprised her. She was used to talking to many guys, but they rarely listened or hung on to her every word the way Jasper did.

"I live in New York, and I travel a lot. It's hard to form meaningful relationships. But you, you would do great on there!"

"I'll think about it," he said, but Brittney knew he only said that to humor her. He had no interest in dating apps.

"I guess you're one of those hopeless romantics," Jasper said in a reflective tone.

Brittney wanted to know what he was thinking. She wanted to know what he thought about her, but she didn't ask. She wasn't here to find a boyfriend. Brittney was here on an assignment to help her best friend plan her dream wedding.

"I love, love. Who doesn't? Dating is hard now, and it's

nothing like it used to be, but I have hope. If love wasn't real, how are Melanie and Cade getting married now? They're perfect for each other," she said.

"That's easy to say when you grow up in a sheltered life with love all around you."

"Sorry, I'm late. I had to do a quick diaper change before coming. Jasper, are you joining us for lunch?" Melanie asked as she took the corner seat.

"I wish I could, but work calls," he said.

"Okay, don't forget I'm taking your headshots for the website today. So, don't leave without coming by the office."

"Maybe we can use one of those for your dating app! We need to tousle your hair a bit and have you unbutton a few of the buttons from your top. Oh, we can do it by the stables. Who doesn't love a sexy cowboy?" Brittney said, excited about the possibility.

Jasper looked mortified just thinking about it. Brittney and Melanie burst out into laughter.

"It sounds like fun," Melanie said and gave Jasper a quick wink.

"You know what? Why not? Let's give it a go," he said as a heart-racing smile spread across his face.

"Why didn't you tell me how cute all these men in Willow Heights are? Maybe I should focus my article on all the eligible bachelors in Willow Heights and how everyone who comes here finds a new beginning and a hot man to go with it," Brittney said once Jasper was gone.

"You met Jasper your first time here and at the engagement party, too." Melanie reminded her.

"Yeah, but the first time I was here, I was dating that French guy, and the second time I was too focused on celebrating you, my very best friend that I love and cherish so much."

"What do you want?" Melanie asked with a raised brow, not missing a beat.

"Well... the magazine wants to feature your wedding," Brittney said, glad to have it out there.

"Why?"

"Why not? You were the best creative director they had. Imagine how gorgeous your wedding will be!"

"I don't think Cade would like that."

"Can you promise that you'll at least consider it? Carol keeps emailing me about it. She'll probably fly down here if I don't convince you."

"I promise to think about it and talk to Cade about it, but that's it."

"That's all I ask. Thank you. Now, let's order because I'm famished."

"Yeah, I've heard flirting with 'sexy cowboys' works up an appetite!" Melanie said teasingly.

* * *

"Hi THERE," Sienna said as Rita opened the door to greet her. Sienna had taken a taxi from the airport since her flight arrived earlier than it was supposed to.

"I'm so glad to see you again. We have missed you. How was Colorado?" Rita asked as she helped Sienna with a small rolling suitcase.

Sienna was a traveling nurse, and her latest assignment had taken her to Colorado.

"It was great. I can't believe my three weeks there are over, but the best part is coming home to you and Bob," Sienna said as they walked to Sienna's room to unpack.

"Little Penny missed you too," Rita said as she placed her corgi dog, Penny, on Sienna's bed.

Penny quickly ran over to Sienna and sat on her lap.

"I guess we will be roommates again, Penny, at least for the two months I'll be in town," Sienna said as she patted Penny's head.

"Two months? That's amazing!" Rita said, overjoyed.

"Yes, I have planned picnics and walks with you, Bob, and Penny."

"I can't wait to spend time with you. I have some special items I'm working on for Melanie's wedding. Now that you are home, you'll be able to help me."

"Great! I'm excited to see the gang. I've missed you all so much. Colorado was beautiful and all, but this is home. This is my happy place."

"Bob's out grocery shopping. He's been waiting for you all day. He wants to make you the best and the only dish he can cook," Rita said with a laugh.

"That is so sweet of him. It's good to be home." Sienna said as she hugged Rita.

"I was waiting to tell you in person. We found a cute little place on Main Street for the jewelry boutique. We can visit tomorrow; they are still vacating the space. It's small and cozy and just perfect for our boutique."

"That's amazing. I can't wait to visit tomorrow. We have to plan how to organize and decorate. It seems like my two months home will be busy," Sienna said, genuinely happy to be a part of Rita's dream come true.

"I hope you don't mind," Rita said.

"Of course not. I'm blessed to be a part of this journey and a new beginning for you. I'm grateful to be here and to receive so much love."

CHAPTER 5

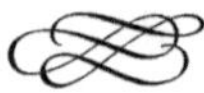

"So, how's the search for your biological dad coming along?" Mary Elle asked DeeAnn.

DeeAnn was off from work today and surprised Mary Elle with a visit to Willow Acres. Mary Elle loved having her sister around; they were long overdue for a meetup. DeeAnn and Mary Elle were currently in Mary Elle's office going over resumes. Now that the inn was up and ready in Willow Acres, they needed to hire staff to run in it. Thomas and David were too busy to look through resumes, so Mary Elle volunteered for the task. Bailey often handled everything to do with human resources and accounting, but her hands were full since it was the end of the month. Mary Elle didn't mind helping. She loved their small team, and sometimes, in a family-owned small business, you needed to wear many hats.

"No luck yet, but I'm staying optimistic."

"I know I wasn't too keen on the idea before, but I hope you find him. I hope you're able to have a relationship with him and that you're able to learn more about that side of your family."

"Thanks, Elle. Your support means a lot to me. I keep envisioning what our first meeting will be like. I keep trying to imagine what he looks like or what he sounds like. But I have to admit; I'm also scared. What if he doesn't want to meet me?"

"What if he does? Who wouldn't want to meet you?"

"I guess we'll find out, eventually. How is Wyatt? Did you tell him Lorraine reached out?"

"We decided not to tell him for now. He's finally in a good place. We started going to church on Sundays as a family, and he's going to youth group. He's making friends and seems genuinely happy."

"I'm glad to hear that. Oh, I think I found someone promising," DeeAnn said as she handed Mary Elle a resume.

Mary Elle took the resume from her and read it over.

"It says here that Omar has 15 years of experience in running an inn, and his last job was in a small inn on the coast of Maine. I think you might have found us our next employee," Mary Elle said excitedly.

Ideally, Mary Elle would have loved to have Tiffany running the Willow Acres Inn, but she was doing so well with Mrs. Adelman that she didn't even dare ask her. Those two made a great team, and Mrs. Adelman had done what Mary Elle had often thought was impossible, getting Tiffany to realize that life was about much more than just work. Tiffany had always been dedicated to school and then worked, but that often left her with no time for much else. Now that she was working with Mrs. Adelman, they both carried the load of running the Inn.

"Should we call him to set up an interview?" DeeAnn asked.

"I want to gather a few more resumes and show them to Thomas before calling anyone, but I think Thomas will like him a lot."

"Sounds like a plan. How are things between you and Thomas now that you're married? Are they the same as before?"

"Things are wonderful. It's difficult to leave work at work, especially since we work together and basically live at work, but he's so great. I can honestly say that I have no complaints. How are things with Paul? We should all have dinner together, and I'll invite Rita and Bob."

"Yes, I would love that. Paul is great. He's thinking of buying a produce farm. It's right next to his tree farm."

"So, he's officially staying in Willow Heights, then? I wasn't sure if he was setting things up at the tree farm before going back home."

Paul had inherited his uncle's Christmas tree farm last year and had moved to Willow Heights temporarily to bring it back to standards. His uncle had let a few things go that needed care, but Paul now had the farm back up and running just like it had during its glory days.

"I'm not sure. I haven't asked him. Mostly because I fear what his answer might be."

"I understand that. You're in a good place right now, and you don't want to rock the boat. Would you consider moving with him?"

"No, this is home, and this is where you are. We spent way too many years apart for me to leave now."

"I would understand if you did. I want you to be happy."

"I am happy. Here with you."

* * *

MELANIE SAT at her desk and massaged her temples. She had fallen behind on getting her clients their wedding photographs out on time. She felt like she was running herself to the ground. It wasn't easy to have a baby, work full time, and plan a wedding. She was eternally grateful for her mother and her experience in planning weddings. Mary Elle was handling most things, which lifted a great weight off Melanie's shoulders. It was hard work balancing life out, but she enjoyed it and was grateful for God's blessings. Ryder stirred in his bassinet that Melanie kept next to her desk. She glanced at the clock and realized Cade would be here any minute now. She wrapped up her work quickly and saved everything.

"Are you ready?" Cade asked Melanie as he softly knocked on her office door. Melanie had been doing her makeup and getting ready to go over the final menu options and taste the meals she had already selected for her wedding night.

"Yes, come in."

"Wow, you look beautiful," Cade said as he gave Melanie a look and planted a sweet kiss on the top of her head.

"Thank you. You're handsome as always. Let's go. Mom is already at the restaurant," Melanie said as she grabbed her purse and Ryder's diaper bag.

"Let me help you with Ryder," Cade said as he picked him up from his bassinet.

Ryder was so loved by Cade; you could never tell he was not Ryder's biological father. Cade had asked Melanie if he could adopt Ryder once they were married. He wanted Ryder to have his last name and never feel like he wasn't part of their family. Melanie, of course, agreed, and needless to say, that melted her heart and made her fall in love with Cade even more, as if that was even possible.

"You made it. I was starting to worry," Mary Elle said as Melanie, Cade, and Ryder walked into the restaurant.

"Sorry, I'm a little late," Melanie said as she parked Ryder's stroller next to their table.

"We will start with tasting everything you already

selected, and if you are not pleased with any of the food items, we can change them," Maurice, the chef, said as he gestured for the server to bring the meals out.

"First, we will begin with the appetizers you selected. Here are the shrimp cocktail shooters, and this one here is the mozzarella and roasted tomatoes," Maurice said as he waited for their comments on the dishes.

"I love the tomatoes," Melanie said as she took another bite. Melanie had always loved tomatoes; they were what she craved the most during her pregnancy with Ryder.

"I love the options," Cade added.

"As do I, exquisite," Mary Elle said with a smile.

"Excellent. Next, we have the soup selections; we have here the roasted butternut squash with whipped cream and maple, and the second soup selected is country leek and potato, parsnip chips."

"Both are delicious," Melanie said.

"I agree as well," Cade said with a small laugh.

"Are you sure, honey?" Melanie asked. She knew Cade would agree with anything she said because he just wanted her to have the wedding of her dreams.

"Yes," he said and kissed the side of her head.

"It's delicious. They are all great selections," Mary Elle said in agreement.

"Here are the salads, mixed greens, carrot, and cucumber with honey apple cider vinaigrette, and the other salad is romaine leaves served with lemon garlic dressing."

"Once again, I love the selections," Melanie said as she finished both samples of salads.

"Well done," Mary Elle added.

"For the main course, you selected the Atlantic roasted salmon with sesame seeds, strips of shitake mushrooms, leeks, and soy-ginger sauce, and the second option selected was the fillet of chicken stuffed with wild rice and cranberry."

"Divine," Melanie said excitedly.

"This is great," Cade said as he stole some of Melanie's little leftovers.

"Very delicious," Mary Elle agreed.

"For desserts, we have the coconut banana verrine, Grand Marnier Misu, and caramel brownie chocolate cheesecakes."

"Beyond delicious," Melanie said, giving Maurice a thumbs up.

"We will also provide the cocktail reception and passed Hors D'oeuvres and coffee and tea."

"Sounds great. I love everything we selected. Could I also add a charcuterie board and cheese station buffet style, of course?" Mary Elle asked Maurice.

"Yes, of course. It would be possible to add a table with this. Will you be adding anything else?"

"Melanie, is there anything you would like to add?" Mary Elle said as she looked over at Melanie.

"I'm ok with everything we have selected and added. Thank you, Maurice."

"Great, it's our pleasure to work with you," Maurice said with a wide smile.

Everything was picture perfect, even better than Melanie had ever dreamed it could be. The next thing she had to do was finalize the bridesmaid dress selection. Tiffany didn't like the dress Melanie had picked out for them, so the girls selected their dresses but had to be in the same color, light peach. Melanie was filled with emotion, trying to finalize her wedding details. She couldn't wait to be Cade's wife. There was another important task on her schedule before the wedding. It was to help Mary Elle plan the rehearsal dinner and squeeze some bonding time with Cade's parents. So much to do and so little time.

As they drove back to Melanie's house, Cade reminded Melanie that they had dinner reservations with both of their parents tomorrow night at the Italian restaurant on Main Street.

"Thanks for reminding me. I thought it was scheduled for next week. I have to remind my mom and Thomas about it. My dad won't be able to join us this time, but he said next time he will be here."

"I'm excited about our families coming together and getting to know each other. I wish they would've had more time to bond before the wedding. But it is what it is."

"Me too," Melanie said, trying to convince herself that she was also excited to know them better.

Melanie felt insecure about their feelings and acceptance of her and Ryder. She felt like they might have wanted Cade to have fallen in love with someone else, someone with less baggage. She was trying to remain optimistic and not let that get in the way of her excitement about the wedding. It could just be her insecurities getting the best of her.

"You don't sound excited," Cade noted as he stole a glance at her.

"I am; I'm just tired," Melanie said while faking a yawn. She pushed her seat back into the reclining position and closed her eyes. She didn't want to get into this right now.

"Yes, it's late. Good thing we are home."

"Oh, I didn't realize we were already here," Melanie said with a small laugh before straightening her seat, "I hope Ryder doesn't wake up as I take him out of the car and put him to bed," Melanie said as Cade opened the car door for her. Melanie couldn't remember the last time she'd opened her door herself. Cade loved opening the doors for her. He was a true gentleman.

"Let me do it; he likes it when I rock him to sleep before

bed," Cade said as he gently unbuckled the car seat and got Ryder out.

"You're so great with him. You are an excellent father," Melanie said as he again caused all the butterflies in her stomach to start a storm in her belly.

Ryder got a little fussy when Cade tried putting him directly into the crib, so Cade took him and sat on the rocking chair in his nursery and rocked him as he hummed Rock A Bye Baby quietly, and Ryder fell back asleep. It was the sweetest sight a mother could ever witness. The love Cade had for them both was otherworldly.

CHAPTER 6

The following day, Melanie worked on editing the headshots for the company website. She also had to write a small paragraph for each employee. Thomas wanted everyone that went on the website to know the faces and names of the team that kept Willow Acres running. Melanie sent Brittney the photos they had taken for Jasper's profile. She wasn't sure why Brittney had taken an interest in finding Jasper a girlfriend. It wasn't like her to do something like that, but she had too much going on right now to decipher what was going on in her friend's mind. Melanie had her office door closed, but she heard a slight commotion outside before her doors swung open.

"Susan! What are you doing here?" Melanie asked as her gaze quickly went to where Ryder was sleeping.

Melanie was always on edge about her mother-in-law showing up and trying to take her son away from her. Susan followed Melanie's gaze, and she walked over to where Ryder was sleeping peacefully in his playpen.

"Is this him?" Susan asked gently.

"Yes," Melanie said, unsure of what to do.

She always imagined that she would tell her to go away if Susan showed up. She would remind her they had no right to her son but seeing Susan here now and how she was looking at Ryder was throwing her for a loop.

"What are you doing here, Susan?" Melanie asked calmly.

Susan turned her gaze to Melanie and straightened her back as if she just remembered the real reason she was here. "I heard you're getting married."

"I am."

"With the man that was at your baby shower?"

"Yes," Melanie said, confused.

"Congratulations, Melanie. May we talk, please?"

"Sure," Melanie said as she went back to her seat. Susan took the chair across from her, and Melanie waited expectantly to hear what she wanted to discuss. Susan opened and closed her mouth a few times, then she stared down at her hands on her lap, saying nothing. Melanie noticed tears slowly streaming down her face.

"What's wrong?" Melanie asked.

Susan glanced up, and their eyes locked. Melanie could see the pain in her eyes, but the older woman still wasn't saying anything.

"Susan, I'm sorry that I haven't answered your calls or messages, but you have to understand. I am trying to make a new life for myself here. Your son wanted nothing to do with me or our baby. He practically threw us out onto the street."

"I know, Melanie. You have every right to keep the baby away from me. I understand that. I discussed this with my lawyers, and I know I could get in trouble for even being here, but I can't help what I am feeling. There's no way to explain it, let alone put it into words. I always liked you, Melanie, and I always believed you deserved better than my son."

"You did?" Melanie asked. She'd always thought Susan disliked her.

"You're noting like my son. You're warm and loving. You come from a great loving family, and it shows. My son never had that. He grew up with nannies. His father and I were always busy trying to keep up with appearances. I know it's my fault. His father grew up the same way, and I should've stood up. I should've taken my place as a mother and wife, but our whole family life was simply a business transaction for his father," Susan said as a small sob escaped her.

Melanie had never seen her like this, so vulnerable and broken. The Susan she knew was always so cold and distant.

"Anyway, I know I deserve nothing from you, Melanie. I want you to know that I am truly sorry that I never let you feel you were a part of our family. I never welcomed you into my heart, and it wasn't because I didn't think you were worthy. I didn't think we deserved you. You didn't fit in because you weren't like us. You didn't have an ulterior motive for being there other than loving my son. I'm sorry for all the pain my family and I caused you. I hope that someday you will forgive me. I would love to have a relation-ship with my grandson," Susan said as she stood and began walking towards the door. She stopped as she passed Ryder, and Melanie thought she would walk over to him again, but she didn't.

"Susan," Melanie said just as soon as Susan was about to walk out.

"Yes?" she said without turning around.

"Would you like to hold him?" Melanie asked.

Susan turned around slowly with tears in her eyes. She nodded. Melanie picked Ryder up and placed him in his grandmother's arms. Susan held him close and sang to him.

Melanie didn't know why she had done this. Before today, she had known that she wanted nothing to do with

Everett or his family, but Susan had come here and apologized, and Melanie couldn't fathom being the one that kept her son away from family. Melanie believed there was always good in people. Everyone could change and learn from their mistakes. Who was she to judge Susan so harshly?

Susan cradled Ryder and gave him kisses on the top of his head.

"He looks like Everett. I wish I could turn back time and show him more love than I did."

"You can't beat yourself up for your mistakes. You can only change the present. Show Everett that you love him, talk with him and tell him what you told me. He needs to hear it too. He needs to know you and his father love him," Melanie said as she watched Susan feel all the love she had hidden inside herself.

"Maybe it's too late. Everett's heart has been so cold towards us now. He's even more distant than ever," Susan said as she gazed at Ryder, who was now fully awake and looking at Susan as if he understood and felt her pain for his father and love for him.

"You'll never know unless you try. You have nothing to lose and everything to gain."

"Thank you for letting me hold him. Could I possibly have a photo of him and me?"

"Of course, let me get my camera," Melanie said as she looked for her camera. Susan handed her a smartphone to take a photo with as well.

"Smile," Melanie said instinctively.

"Again, thank you, Melanie. I am sorry for barging in here. I just needed to see Ryder. I wasn't expecting to get so much time with him as you have allowed me to have today."

"It's ok; I understand you needed to see him."

"Congratulations on your upcoming wedding. I hope

Cade deserves you. You are truly a very special lady," Susan said as she walked out of Melanie's office.

What a day it had been. Melanie felt terrible to see the pain Susan was in for all her parental mistakes. Being a parent wasn't easy, especially when your childhood was not great and your parents displayed the same behaviors. It was a cycle that needed to be broken, and healing needed to occur in everyone's hearts.

* * *

BRITTNEY SAT AT THE OVERLOOK, admiring the vast greatness of the mountains. She took a deep, long breath and tried to settle her thoughts. She rarely had moments like these where she was left alone with nothing but her thoughts. Being in Willow Heights gave her a lot of time to self-reflect and thought about every detail of her life. Brittney had thought about reaching out to her mother but then decided against it. She knew better than that, she thought as she wiped a tear from her face.

Seeing Melanie with Mary Elle always resurfaced feelings that she often tried to ignore. Since a young age, she'd always wanted a close relationship with her mother, but her mother, Alice, was never the motherly kind. Brittney filled that void with her grandmother, Amelia. Brittney and Amelia did everything together. Her grandmother taught her how to sew and cook, and she even taught her how to drive a car. When her grandmother passed away, she felt alone in the world.

That was when she started blogging and reinvented herself. No one wanted to follow the life of a sad girl from a small town in Kansas, so she became this fashionista who traveled and ate all kinds of foods worldwide. She created a great life for herself, but that life often left her feeling empty.

Brittney didn't have any real friends because she could never be her true self. She was always playing a role, and no one knew the real Brittney. Not even Melanie knew what her life in Kansas had been like.

"Are you okay?" Jasper asked. He was carrying a medkit, and a dog was trailing after him.

"Yes, I'm okay. Who is this?" Brittney asked as she scratched the dog beneath his chin.

"This is Coop. David brought him over around Christmas time, something about Willow Acres needing a resident dog."

"He's adorable. Like you in those photos, Melanie sent me for your profile."

"Ah, I had forgotten about that. You weren't kidding, were you?"

"I never kid around about dating apps. Plus, I need something to keep me busy while Melanie's at work. I'm going stir crazy."

"Well, our girl Helen has been trying to push out a calf for the last few hours with no luck. I think it's time I step in. Want to join me? Then we can go have dinner and set up these profiles you keep hammering me about."

"Sure, lead the way," she said, and they took off to the barn.

Once inside the barn, Jasper introduced Brittney to the curly-haired cow.

"Brittney, this is my main girl, Helen. Helen, this is Brittney. She'll be helping deliver your baby today," Jasper said as he rolled up his sleeves and knelt next to the cow.

"Hi Helen," Brittney said as she knelt on the other side of the cow and gently petted her.

Jasper went quiet as he examined Helen. Brittney didn't say a thing. She felt completely out of place.

"We're going to have to pull. I think I can do it on my own, but you should prep too, just in case."

"Prep?"

"Yes, first we'll wash from our hands up to our shoulders. I'll give you an extra pair of gloves. I'll apply lubricant on mine, but not yours."

"Okay," Brittney said as she followed Jasper to the sink and followed his directions.

They went back to their positions next to Helen. Jasper tried pushing the calf's legs back but wasn't able to. He then tied a rope around the calf's legs and pulled it out. Brittney saw he was struggling, and before he could ask for help, she pulled as well. It might have only been seconds or minutes, but it felt like hours when they could finally pull the calf out.

Jasper cleaned it up, but it wasn't breathing. He extended its neck and began to blow into its nose. That didn't work, so he did sternum simulations and chest pumps, hoping to have the calf expel whatever it had aspirated during labor. When all hope seemed to be lost, the small calf coughed. It kept coughing, and after each cough, it seemed to improve. They sat there with the calf and Helen, waiting for it to stand and take its first step, but nothing happened. Jasper told Britney he would milk out the colostrum, the first milk produced by the mother after birth, as it's vital for the calf. Jasper showed Britney how to give the colostrum to the calf.

"Is it going to be okay?" she asked him with tears in her eyes. She had experienced nothing like this before.

"Yes, I believe so," Jasper said as he rubbed the small calf.

When the small calf stood and took a couple of wobbly steps towards its mother, Brittney began to cry.

"I bet you never delivered a calf before in any of your travels," Jasper said as he bumped his shoulder to hers.

"I am always going to remember this. Thank you for inviting me. I should probably go to the Inn to take a long shower now."

"Shower sounds nice. I can't leave yet. My car is at the shop and David isn't back yet. He's my ride."

"I can drop you off."

"Are you sure?"

"Yes, I rented a red convertible because I wanted to drive in the Blue Ridge with my top-down with the girls, but my friends are now in love and boring."

"We can't have you not live out your dream," Jasper said seriously.

"I know, right?"

"Let's shower and then go for a drive?"

"I'm so glad I have a new friend here," Brittney said as she wrapped her arms with Jasper, and they walked over to her bright red convertible.

CHAPTER 7

"*L*ivy, daddy's home!" Tiffany called out to the small dog as soon as she heard David's motorcycle outside.

Tiffany picked Livy up and held her as she opened the door for David. Livy was still very apprehensive around others, specifically men, but Tiffany had noticed that if she held the dog while inviting guests in, she was usually more welcoming.

"Were you two waiting for me?" David asked as he came up the front porch steps.

He pulled a treat out of his pocket and slowly held out his palm, a treat for Livy to take. The dog growled but quickly stopped at the sight of the treat. She gingerly took the treat from his hand. Tiffany then placed her on the floor, and the dog scurried off to enjoy her treat.

"Someone's warming up to you."

"To me or the treats?"

"Well, I'm definitely warming up to you," Tiffany said as she pulled him closer by his jacket.

"Are you?" David asked as he took a step closer.

"Get a room, you two!" Melanie said as she playfully pushed them out of the doorway on her way to the kitchen.

"Mel! I didn't hear you arrive," Tiffany said as she felt her face heating up.

Cade came up the porch steps with Ryder in his arms and Brittney close behind.

"I'm so excited about game night!" Brittney said, and Tiffany hoped she hadn't heard her small exchange with David.

"Can you believe she's never played Jenga?" Jasper asked as he came up the steps holding four boxes of pizzas.

Tiffany hadn't been expecting him but was happy to see that he was socializing with the group. He was always alone, and apart from events at Willow Acres, she never really saw him around.

"This is a delightful surprise. I wasn't expecting a game night tonight. Oh, pizza! Yum," Tiffany said as she and David walked towards the living room.

"You guys won't believe what I did with Jasper," Brittney said as everyone turned to look at her and Jasper.

"What did you do?" Melanie asked.

"I helped him deliver a calf. Helen was having difficulties with her birth. At first, it was scary seeing that the calf wasn't moving or breathing. Then, with Jasper's expertise, he gave the calf mouth to mouth breathing, and it coughed, and then it was breathing. It was incredible to have witnessed it," Brittney told her story with so much passion that it captured their attention.

"After that, we gave the calf the colostrum because it wasn't walking around yet; it was still fragile. But right after it drank it, the calf got up and walked over to Helen," Jasper continued, telling their amazing story.

"Wow, what an adventure Brit," Melanie said.

"I'll never forget it, and Helen was so grateful for all of

Jasper's help," Brittney said as she looked at Jasper, who was blushing since he was not used to having so much attention from a crowd.

"That's why Jasper is my go-to man," David said proudly.

"That's wonderful, Jasper. You have so much experience," Tiffany added.

"I'm just glad Helen and the calf are doing well now," Jasper said with a bright smile.

"He's modest and doesn't like the attention," Brittney said as he was still blushing. "I'll have to add that he's modest, quick on his feet, and great with pets to his dating profile."

"Dating profile?" David asked.

"Yeah, Brittney and Melanie have convinced me to meet women online," Jasper said sourly.

"Dude, I didn't know you were up for dating," Cade chimed in.

"Well, I guess I am now open to dating again," Jasper said, with cheeks even brighter than red Christmas lights.

"I know this girl that works at my firm that is available," Cade said.

"You mean Martha?" Jasper asked.

"Yeah, you know her?"

"Sure do. She's a lot to handle," Jasper said while setting up the Jenga pieces.

"Well, I guess that's that," Cade said with a small laugh.

"The pizza is served, guys," Melanie called out from the kitchen.

"We also have frozen margaritas and beers," Tiffany offered from the kitchen.

"It feels like a sleepover, except we are older and don't need chaperones," Melanie told Tiffany while she took a margarita and her slices of pizza.

"This is nice. We should do this more often," Tiffany said

as she gestured to Melanie to click her margarita glass with hers.

Mary Elle and Thomas dropped by for a few minutes to pick up Ryder. They were taking him to watch a school play with them and would watch him for the rest of the night. Once they finished eating, the group moved to the living room, where they played Jenga.

"I guess you're a natural," Melanie whispered in Brittney's ear as she took her turn.

"Don't distract me, Mel. This is like performing surgery!" Brittney said with a giggle.

"Don't drop the tower, don't drop the tower," Tiffany said, making Brittney nervous.

"I can't hear you. I can't hear you," Brittney chanted back at Tiffany.

To everyone's surprise, Brittney was able to make her move without knocking down the tower. They took turns, and as the pieces dwindled, the tension in the room elevated.

"Is that sweat on your forehead?" Tiffany asked David with an evil laugh as he pulled a piece out.

"Tiff, a win for me is a win for you," David told her as he dragged the piece out with ease.

"There are no teams in Jenga, babe."

The banter between the group went on for the rest of the night. Melanie ended up being the one to make the pieces fall.

"So, did you speak with Cade about featuring the wedding in the magazine?" Brittney asked Melanie as the guys tried picking a movie for them all to watch.

"Yeah, we spoke about it, but he's not sure how it works. Are they writing a piece on our story and how we are now getting married, or is it just about Willow Heights and their vendors and places to get married? Like, how deep into our business are you digging?" Melanie asked as she turned to face Brittney.

"Carol wants some juicy bits. You know how she is, but I want to focus on Willow Heights and everything it offers brides regarding locations, venues, vendors, and the whole enchilada. So, I guess the answer to your question is a little of both," Brittney said as sincerely as she could answer Melanie.

"How cool would it be to have your wedding featured, though?" Tiffany asked.

"But why me? I'm no celebrity and far from being an influencer."

"The magazine wants to feature more normal women."

"Let me discuss it with Cade again now that we know the angle for this feature. But keep in mind that I don't want any personal details out there. I don't think Everett will ever read or care about me moving on, but I don't want to start any drama with Susan. She can be a little scary." Melanie told Brittney.

"I know, I understand. Trust me, I don't want to write a gossip piece. I want the world to know that you are an amazing woman with a great love story. You found your happy ending. I want to give other women who might be experiencing the same that you did hope for the future. Love is a beautiful thing, and it's out there, and I want the readers to know that."

* * *

AFTER A VERY SUCCESSFUL GAME NIGHT, Cade drove Melanie home. It had been a long time since Melanie had a child-free night. She loved Ryder and never took her time with him for granted, but it was nice to have a night off. There was no denying that being a mother was hard. It took a toll on her physically, mentally, and social life. This night was the first time Melanie enjoyed herself and could enjoy the night without worrying about feeding Ryder or changing any diapers. She almost felt like her old self again, but she felt guilty that she wasn't spending time with him. She'd heard about mom guilt before, but now that she was experiencing it, she knew how hard it was.

"Did you get to ask Brittney about the magazine feature?" Cade asked, cutting into her thoughts.

"Yes, she explained that Carol, my old boss at the magazine, wanted a juicy piece. But Brittney said she wanted to focus on Willow Heights and everything that Willow Heights offers couples looking to get married out in the countryside."

"That might be good for the town, right?" Cade said as he quickly took his eyes off the road to glance at her.

"Yeah, Brittney also said she would write about us but would not go into too much personal detail about our relationship. What do you think?" Melanie asked Cade.

"I told you, Mel, I'm ok with it if you are. As long as I get to call you my wife at the end of this," Cade said as he took Melanie's hand and kissed it.

"I can't wait to be your wife!" Melanie said, unable to keep from smiling.

"Me too."

The car ride was quick since everyone lived nearby. Cade quickly jumped out of the car and opened the door for Melanie. He offered her his hand for support before getting out of his truck.

"Thanks for game night. It was a great idea," Melanie said as they walked to her front door.

"Ryder is sleeping over at Mary Elle's?"

"Just for tonight. It's so late. I didn't want to keep my mom waiting for me or wake her up to go get him," Melanie said as she opened the door.

Cade stepped inside to ensure it was safe, the same way

he always did. Those little details always melted Melanie's heart.

"I'll see you tomorrow morning," Cade said as he gave her a goodbye kiss on her lips.

"Text me when you get home. I love you," Melanie called out as he got in his car.

He gave her a small wave and drove off. This was the first night Melanie was alone at home without Ryder. She was exhausted from a long day at work, and the great game night they just had. Melanie opted to change into her pajamas and head to bed. She received Cade's text confirming he had made it home and the wonderful 'I love you' included, which still gave her butterflies in her stomach. She couldn't wait to marry the man of her dreams and begin a new life together with him. Melanie knew Cade shared many, if not all, of her same values and goals in life. She knew God placed him in her life, and she always thanked him for giving her the strength to move on and not give up on life and love.

As Melanie lay in bed, she couldn't stop thinking about what Britney had said about her story motivating others. She didn't want to share too much of her story with Everett out of respect for him, but she knew Brittney was right. There were many women trapped in toxic and abusive relationships that might not know that there is light at the end of the tunnel, no matter how dark and long that tunnel might be. Melanie also knew that she wasn't the one who got herself out of that relationship but that God had always been by her side and had led and protected her. It was all so much to think about and contemplate.

Before drifting off to dreamland, Melanie prayed and included a special prayer for all the women who might be in a terrible situation and asked God to send them help and guidance so they, too, could overcome the same way she had.

* * *

"Guess what!" Brittney said as she walked into the barn where Jasper was working.

"You won the lottery?" he asked with a mischievous grin.

"No, silly. Last night, I set up your dating apps, and you already have quite a few matches!"

"Oh my God! No way!" Jasper said in mock excitement.

Brittney rolled her eyes and said, "Trust the process. I will find you love before I go back to New York. I can promise you that."

"Tell me, how did I become your pet project?" Jasper asked with a raised brow and a sly smile.

"I don't know. I like you, Jasper. You seem like a great guy. Why should you be alone?" Brittney said with a shrug.

She really couldn't explain why she was trying to help him. It made little sense to her. She kept telling herself it was because she was trying to find something to keep herself busy while here. She told herself it was not because she enjoyed his company and found him easy to talk to. Jasper wasn't like the guys she was used to. She didn't feel like she had to pretend to have a big and exciting life with him. She could just be herself, and that was something she hadn't been in a long time.

"I'm happy the way I am," he said as he continued with his work.

"Where are you from, anyway? Did you grow up here? Where is your family?" Brittney asked as she propped herself up on a workbench.

"My dad was in the army, so I moved around a lot. My grandmother lived here in Willow Heights for many years. I came to visit her for a summer, and I never returned home. I don't keep in contact with my parents. My dad could never understand why I wouldn't want to follow in his footsteps.

What's your story, Brittney? Where are you from?" Jasper said as he turned his attention over to her.

"I grew up in Kansas. I was an only child, and I moved to New York as soon as possible."

"What about your family?"

"I never knew my father, and my mom still lives in Kansas. Oh, look! You have a new match," she said as she showed him the notification on her phone.

Brittney showed him her profile and her photos. She seemed like a nice girl. She wasn't from Willow Heights, but Winding Creek wasn't very far. Brittney was glad for the distraction. She wasn't ready to bare her soul to anyone. Some things were better left unknown, like her relationship with her mother.

"Should we ask her out on a date?" Brittney asked.

"We just matched a minute ago. We haven't even talked."

"You need to move fast if you want to get anywhere. Meet first and text later. Otherwise, you'll spend all this time texting, and it might just not work out when you finally meet."

"Okay, you're the pro," Jasper said and quickly got back to work.

"I set the date up for tonight at seven. You're meeting her at that cool gastropub we went to. I'll be back at five, so I can help you get ready."

"Is that necessary? I know how to dress."

"I know, but first impressions are everything," Brittney said as she hopped off the workbench and went off before he could try to sway her anymore.

She took her time getting back to Melanie's office. She walked by the lake and sat under a tree, where she spent a few minutes journaling. For some reason, being in Willow Heights made her feel less lonely. She realized that not everyone was vain and materialistic and that people could be happy without having to show and pretend to be happy. Brittney didn't have to post on social media about her day to enjoy it. She didn't feel the need to get validation for her day or level of accomplishment while she was here. She understood that being an influencer and even writing could positively impact someone's life without having to go outward of yourself. Happiness was not based on someone else's perception of it or having to prove you were happy by posting selfies with expensive things and fake smiles.

It had been a long time since Brittney had enjoyed herself so much that she didn't have to glance at her phone to see how many "likes," "follows," or "friend requests" she had received. She was present at the moment, and she enjoyed getting to know everyone on a deeper level. Even her relationship with Melanie was getting better. She wasn't ready to go back to New York, and she wondered if she even wanted to. No matter how exciting or adventurous her life may have seemed, she was lonely. All her relationships were empty, and her agent set most up. The only friend that expected nothing from her was Melanie. Could she walk away from it all? Did she really want to?

CHAPTER 8

"You finally made it back," Melanie said with a hint of suspicion in her tone when Brittney walked into her office.

"I talked to Jasper, and he got some matches on the app. He's going on a date tonight," Brittney said proudly.

Melanie knew Brittney prided herself on her matchmaking abilities. She often said there wasn't a better cupid than her.

"That's great, and how does Jasper feel about dating this girl? Do they have things in common?"

"Well, he's only seen her photo and profile, but I'm sure he will discover what they have in common tonight over dinner," Brittney said with a shrug.

"Dating has changed so much. I'm glad I wasn't meeting random men like that."

"Welcome to the future, I guess."

"So, I spoke with Cade about the magazine feature. We will agree to be featured only if it's based more on the wedding vendors, Willow Heights, and less on the details of our love story. I don't want any comparisons between Cade and Everett, and no bad-mouthing Everett. I don't want anyone thinking negatively about him."

"You can read it and change the article before I submit it to Carol. Whatever you don't feel comfortable with can be edited out."

"Ok, then you can feature our wedding. It would be nice to have a small piece about David's animal sanctuary. It will be open to the public soon. He could use the publicity and maybe get sponsorship."

"Yeah, I was thinking about that. Our readers love animals, too, and I'm sure someone can sponsor David. I'll ask David if he's ok with it and when he will do the grand opening for the sanctuary."

"Thanks, Brittney; you do not know how much this will help him. He's taken on a lot because he loves those animals, and he's given it his all, literally."

"I know, and I'll help him as much as possible."

"How are you liking Willow Heights?" Melanie asked Brittney curiously since this had been the longest that Brittney had stayed in Willow Heights. Coming from a big city with many events, people, and the hustle and bustle, she was curious to know how Brittney was holding up.

"I have to admit, this is a languid pace for me, but I feel like not rushing through is re-energizing me. I have been able to write in my journal finally. I've been doing a lot of self-reflecting and going within and analyzing different aspects of me, of who I am and what I want."

"Wow, that's deep. I'm so glad you could disconnect from all the outside distractions and reconnect with yourself on a deeper level. It happened to me too. My life goals have changed, and I feel like I'm living now. The rushing and deadlines are not my drive anymore."

"I feel like I can breathe. I can be myself and not have to seek validation based on brands and stuff."

Melanie had noticed that Brittney seemed much more relaxed and happier than before.

"I feel like some of the heaviness I had been carrying around for so long is being lifted, and kind of like I'm setting myself free," Brittney said, and Melanie could tell she was having a hard time explaining what she was feeling. But she understood her because she had felt the same way not too long ago.

"I know exactly what you mean. I'm here for you always. I love you just the way you are, Brittney. You're my best friend and have been there for me even when I wasn't answering my emails and calls. I never got to thank you for that; thanks for being a great friend." Melanie said as she hugged Brittney.

"You're welcome. I knew you were dealing with things and needed space. I'm so happy that you got your life back on track and found someone amazing to love you and Ryder. You've been an example for me in many ways, and I hope to grow and become a better version of myself."

"You will. God will guide you."

"You know I've always had problems and differences with my mom, but I'm working on that relationship with her. You and Mary Elle are so connected and loving towards each other. I want that with my mother. She's all I got left now."

Brittney didn't speak very often of her mother or her life back in Kansas. A few times, she'd let Melanie in on a few things. Melanie wished she would open up more to her, but she didn't pressure her. She wasn't ready, and that was okay.

"You will have a close relationship with her. Sometimes you have to learn to forgive and let go. My relationship with my mom hasn't always been perfect. I knew she didn't like Everett, and eloping was my way of 'getting back at her,' but that wasn't the right thing to do for her or myself. But she was always there for me; no matter what happens in your life or what decisions you make, she will always love you and be there for you when you need her. It's what moms do. I didn't understand it before, but when I was pregnant with Ryder, those maternal instincts kicked in, and understanding of why my mom was in certain ways with me and my siblings began to make sense. As a mother, you have this responsibility for the baby you are bringing into this world, and the love you feel is so immense that no matter what they do wrong or hurtful, you will always love them. No relationship is perfect. It's just a love relationship you have with your child. This is why I'm more than certain that if you reach out to her, she will be there for you."

"Thanks, Mel, you've given me the push I needed to reach out to her. I know she loves me. I love her dearly; she's my mother. I want to make things better with her."

"I'm so excited for you. Maybe she can come to the wedding?"

"We'll see how things progress."

* * *

BRITTNEY SAT on Jasper's tan leather sofa as she waited for him to shower. She was excited to have him going on this date. Not one to sit still for long, she began to look around the place. It was a small two-bedroom home, but its open floor plan made it seem much bigger. It was your typical bachelor pad. There were no photographs or artwork on the walls, but the few things that were there; she could tell he had picked out carefully.

"Did I pass the test?" Jasper asked as he walked out of his room.

"The test?"

"You're checking out my place. Does it meet your standards?"

"I'm not sure what I was expecting, but it's nice. It's spotless, which is a kind of surprising."

"Hey! Do I look like a slob?" Jasper asked with a hand over his heart and a glint in his eye.

"No, of course not. But you are a boy, so."

"What about my outfit? Do I get a pass there?"

Brittney took a moment to look him over. He was wearing black jeans, a white t-shirt, and a black leather jacket, which his broad shoulders filled in perfectly. He had styled his hair back and smelled divine.

"You look great, Jasper. There's going to be one very lucky lady tonight."

"It's only our first date, Brit. Geez."

"I didn't mean it like that!" Brittney said, and her cheeks started to heat up.

"I know. I'm joking. So, what's the plan? Are you staying here till I come back? Are you going to be watching me while on my date?"

"No. You should go and have a great time. I'll meet you at Willow Acres tomorrow, where you can tell me all about it, but I need a ride to the Inn. Can you drop me off on your way?" Brittney asked as she gathered her things and followed Jasper out.

"Of course," he said.

Jasper locked up his house, then walked over to his car, where he opened the door for her and waited until she was comfortably seated inside before closing the door. The car smelled just like Jasper, woodsy and manly. His car had seen better days. The paint outside was a little rusted, and the leather seats were peeling, but she didn't feel out of place.

"Well, here we are," Jasper said as he stopped his car in front of the Inn, and Tiffany waved from the door.

"Thanks for the ride. Have fun!" Brittney said as she got out of the car and was greeted by Tiffany.

"No, thank you for helping me get ready. I hope this date

goes well," Jasper said as Brittney closed the car door and waved goodbye.

Mrs. Adelman was at the front desk when Brittney and Tiffany walked into the Inn.

"That's the smile of a girl in love," Mrs. Adelman said as she watched Brittney closely.

"In love? Maybe with life? I've never felt more relaxed than I have this past week."

"Willow Heights has a way of doing that," Tiffany said as she offered Brittney a piece of cornbread.

"This is so good!"

"It's my special recipe. It has honey and feta cheese."

"Mm, very nice, Mrs. A," Tiffany said as she grabbed another small piece.

"Was that Jasper dropping you off? You two have been spending a lot of time together," Tiffany noted.

"Yes, I helped him get ready for his date. I like Jasper. He reminds me of home. He's a lot like my guy friends from back home, not like the guys in New York."

"Jasper is a great guy. His grandmother was a very dear friend of mine," Mrs. Adelman said.

"He is. So, Tiff, what are we doing for Melanie's bachelorette party?"

"I think she and Cade want to have their last hurrah together."

"Really?" Brittney asked, scrunching up her nose.

"Yeah, I think it's kind of sweet."

"I guess. I was hoping for a fun girl's weekend, but I keep forgetting how boring couples can be," Brittney said jokingly.

"We can still have fun with the guys. Who knows, maybe one of them gets drunk enough to do a lap dance," Tiffany joked as Mrs. Adelman laughed at the idea of seeing the guys getting wild.

"I wouldn't mind," Brittney said with a giggle.

CHAPTER 9

"Mary Elle?" Wyatt said as he called her at work.

"Hi Wyatt, is everything ok, sweetheart?" Mary Elle asked as she could sense a bit of sadness in his tone of voice.

"I'm ok. I just got home after spending some time with Molly."

"That's nice. How is Molly?" Mary Elle asked as she checked her calendar on her desktop computer.

"She broke up with me."

"Aw, sweetie. I'm sure things will work out, don't worry. Are you going to basketball practice today?"

Mary Elle had feared this might be happening. Molly had just started college after taking a year off. It was understandable that she would want to meet new people.

"Yes, I'm getting ready. I'm just sad that she broke up with me," Wyatt said, and Mary Elle could tell that he was crying. Her heart broke for him, but she was glad that he called her and was opening up.

"I know, honey. Did she say why?"

"No, she just said she wanted to see other guys."

"Maybe she needs time to be alone and think about things. You were a good friend to her, and I'm sure she knows that."

There was silence for a few seconds, and then she could tell that Wyatt was crying. He loved Molly, and this was his first girlfriend. She wanted to be home and hug him tight and take away his pain, but she was at work.

"Sweetie, I'll be there soon," Mary Elle said as she hung up and looked for Thomas.

"Hello, beautiful," Thomas said as she met with him in the parking lot where Thomas parked his truck after going out for supplies to run.

"Hi, honey. Wyatt just called, and he's upset because Molly broke up with him." Mary Elle said in a rushed and urgent tone.

"Is he ok?" Thomas asked as he began to pull bags out of his truck.

"He was crying. He said he was upset about it. I wanted to know if I could leave work early and make sure he's ok and drive him to basketball practice and stop for ice cream or something on the way back home after."

"Yes, of course, you can go. He needs you," Thomas said with a small smile and a gentle squeeze on Mary Elle's shoulder.

"Thanks, I love you. See you at home," Mary Elle said before kissing him.

* * *

THOMAS AND JASPER had just finished unloading his truck with the supplies when Melanie and Brittney stopped by.

"Is mom ok? She left in a hurry." Melanie asked Thomas.

"Yes, she's ok. Wyatt and Molly broke up, and he called her upset. She went to check on him."

"Oh, ok, I hope he's ok. I know breaking up is difficult," Melanie said.

"The first heartbreak is always the worst," Brittney said.

"Yes, it is, and he already has so much going on. But I'm confident that Mary Elle will help him feel better. She has a way with people," Thomas said.

"Isn't that the truth," Melanie said with a laugh.

"Let me help you," Brittney said to Jasper as she saw him struggling to carry too many things at once.

"Long time no talk," Brittney said once they were alone in the barn.

"It's been a busy morning," Jasper said as he began to put things away.

"How was the date?"

"It was great. Kathy, my date, was very nice, and we talked about animals most of the night," Jasper said as he walked toward the barn, and Brittney followed him.

"That's great. She's an animal lover like you. Are you going to have a second date?"

"I haven't called her after last night's date. I've been busy with work."

"You didn't call her or text her today?"

"Nope, not yet."

"Did you like her at all?"

"She's very attractive, and we like animals, but I don't think we have anything else in common. I don't think I would want to go on a second date."

Brittney didn't know why, but hearing Jasper say that sped her heart up.

"I'll check the app to see if there are any other matches," Britney said as she rolled her eyes. She never understood why men were so disconnected from their feelings.

"I can't go on dates tonight or tomorrow," Jasper said in a serious tone.

"Oh, why not?" Brittney asked. She hoped she wasn't being too pushy and annoying him.

"I'm helping David at the sanctuary. He wants to have the grand opening soon."

"Oh, yes, Melanie asked me to include a small article about his sanctuary to help him get the animals adopted and maybe some vendor sponsorships."

"That would be awesome. David has spent almost all his life savings on the sanctuary. He bought the land and built the barn, and he's paying for all the food, medication, and supplies to keep it running."

"I know. Melanie told me about it. He's got a big heart."

"He does. Some of the animals are severely sick or need long-term care, and he's there helping them. It's not an easy task."

"I didn't know some animals needed long-term care. I just thought they would heal."

"Some animals get diabetes, renal failure, kidney stones, just like humans. Some need surgery or casts or IVs. He's lucky to have Lindsay helping him too. She's from Winding Creek, but she comes once a month to check on the animals to make sure everyone is ok."

"That's great. What if there's an emergency?"

"She would come, or David could take the animals to her."

"Right, that makes sense."

"I can do the basics, but for emergencies, we need Lindsay."

"Oh, I see. David's lucky to have you as well."

Jasper blushed and looked away. Brittney loved how modest he was.

"Maybe you can join us? For your article?" Jasper asked.

"Yeah, sounds like a good idea."

Brittney was finding it difficult to be around Jasper. He was handsome and sweet. She was starting to realize she might have a slight crush on him. But she wasn't sure how he felt about her. He probably thought she was a shallow person. Most people didn't take her seriously because of her lifestyle. Brittney had been content with being single and keeping to herself until she started spending time with him. He just made it so easy to be herself. Did he realize she was different than the girl she showed everyone else?

"Well, I got to get back to work," Jasper told Brittney as he took Sunshine out of the barn and fit her for a saddle.

"I'll be here until Melanie leaves, in case you need me," Brittney said as she noticed a change in his attitude and wondered if she had offended him somehow.

CHAPTER 10

With only a month before the wedding, Melanie got a little nervous about everything going smoothly. She and Cade decided that they didn't want a long engagement. They wanted to get married before the busy season in the summer so that they could take two weeks off for a honeymoon. Brittney already had her part of the feature about their love story, and Melanie had taken several photographs of the small details like their rings, the invitations, the flowers, the wedding dress, Ryder's outfit, Cade's shoes, just pictures of the small details that meant a lot to Melanie. Some photos were just for her, but she also took some for Brittney to feature.

"Hi is this Melanie?" a voice said as Melanie answered an unknown number.

"Yes, this is she. Who is this?"

"Hi, it's Tina calling you about your wedding cake order."

"Okay, is there a problem with my order?"

"Unfortunately, we can't accommodate your order as we've lost two of our bakers and haven't found replacements for them yet, and we have a lot of backorders."

"That is so unprofessional."

"I'm truly sorry. I know your wedding is two weeks away, but that is why I'm calling you. Also, a refund of your deposit has already been made."

Melanie was furious and didn't know what to do with so little time left for her wedding, and now there was no cake. She tried to calm down and speak with her mom, but she was in a meeting. Where else could she get her dream cake done with such short notice? She could ask Lisa, but she didn't want to overwhelm her. She knew she was making the cakes for the other weddings that Mary Elle was hosting.

Would Brittney be able to help her find another bakery that would make her beautiful cake on time?

There was a knock on her office door, and Molly popped her head in.

"Hi Melanie, Claire is here to see you about the wedding."

"Claire?" Melanie asked, confused.

"Yes, she says she's your wedding planner."

"My mother is my wedding planner."

Molly stood there, unsure of what to say.

"Okay, send her in."

Melanie looked through her emails to see if maybe they had a client named Claire. Perhaps Molly had misunderstood her?

"Melanie?" said a beautiful, elegantly dressed young woman.

"Yes, welcome," Melanie said as she went over to her and shook her hand.

"I am so excited to be here. I've heard so much about you," Claire said.

"Thank you. I think there's a bit of confusion. Molly said you're a wedding planner?"

"Yes, the magazine sent me here for your wedding. Did no one tell you I was coming?"

"No. I already have a wedding planner. My mother plans all the weddings here."

"I see. I'm sure your mother is an amazing planner, but I think the magazine wants something more refined, which is where I come in. I've planned weddings for some of the top celebrities, and I can assure you that I will plan the wedding of your dreams."

"I understand, and thank you for coming, but this is just a misunderstanding."

"The magazine is going to pay for my services. They will also pay for your wedding. They want it to be one of a kind. They have some special guests coming, and they need to show off."

"Claire, thank you for coming. I'm sorry the magazine made you come all this way and wasted your time. I'm sure you're very talented, but we've got everything under control," Melanie said as she stood, hoping that Claire would get the point.

Claire smiled warily and made her way out. Melanie couldn't believe the magazine had sent a wedding planner when they knew she was having her mother handle that. Melanie grabbed her phone and went in search of Brittney.

It didn't take long to find Brittney. She was sitting at her usual spot near the lake. Melanie had never been upset at Brittney before, but today, she was fuming.

"Hey Mel, I've been working on the story all morning. I can't wait for you to read what I've added. I think you're going to like it."

"Why didn't you tell me the magazine was sending a wedding planner? Didn't you tell them my mother was handling that? And what did they mean by wanting something more refined? It's my wedding!"

"Whoa, calm down. I have no idea what you're talking about. Carol mentioned having a friend that was a wedding planner to the stars, but I told her Mary Elle was planning it. I didn't know she would send someone. I swear."

"What did they mean by more refined? What have you told them?"

"I didn't tell them anything. Carol didn't like the idea of having it in a small town. She thought it should be in New York. She wanted a big, fancy wedding, but I reminded her that our readers want something they can relate to."

"Britt, this is my wedding. I never asked to be in a magazine or anything of this sort. Please, speak to Carol and tell her I am not interested in the magazine butting into my wedding."

"Got it. Understood. I'm sorry, Mel. I really had no idea."

"It's okay, Britt."

Melanie should've known better than to think that Brittney was in on this. Brittney was her one true friend, and she shouldn't have gone off on her like that. Melanie was still working on controlling herself and her outbursts. It had been a very long time since she'd been so upset. She just didn't like having strangers come and tell her how to run her wedding. All she wanted was a private event with those closest to her. If she had learned anything at all in the last few years, it was that nothing mattered in life more than love. Having a big, fancy wedding might have interested her before, but now she knew all she needed was her family and the man she loved.

* * *

BRITTNEY AND JASPER were at what had become their usual hangout spot, the barn. Brittney was currently petting Helen as Jasper examined her. Helen hadn't been feeling well since she'd gone into labor the week before.

"Do you think she's okay?" Brittney asked.

She never thought she would be so invested in a cow's life, but here she was. Willow Heights was getting to her, and she didn't mind it one bit. She loved the slower-paced life. Her agent had been messaging her about brand deals and the need to keep her profile going, but she didn't have the mental capacity to deal with that right now.

"I think so, but I'd rather have Lindsay come check her out to be sure," Jasper said.

Brittney could tell there was something wrong by his tone.

"What's wrong, Jasper?"

"Nothing, don't worry about it," he said and stormed out of the barn before she could press him again.

Brittney ran after him and found him leaning against the fence.

"Jasper, what's wrong? Please tell me."

"I failed her, Britt. I've been so distracted that I wasn't keeping a close watch on her. If anything happens to Helen, it's my fault."

"That's not true. I've seen the way you care for her. She's been doing fine all this time! Today is the first day that she really doesn't look well. Lindsay will come and check her out. Don't beat yourself up," Brittney said and placed a hand on his arm.

Jasper stared down at where her hand rested on him. This small act seemed intimate, and she slowly pulled her hand away. What was she doing?

"Here she is!" Mary Elle said as she rounded the corner.

Brittney's ex-boyfriend, Chase, followed close behind her.

"Chase! What are you doing here?" Brittney asked as she got up and walked over to them.

Chase looked entirely out of place. He was wearing a pink polo shirt with colorful Bermuda shorts and fisherman shoes. His hair was perfectly styled, and his eyebrows were perfectly waxed. Brittney looked down at her shorts and dirty sneakers and wondered what he might think. She wasn't even wearing make-up today, and her hair was probably a mess.

"You've barely been posting since you got here. I wanted to make sure you were okay," he said as he wrapped an arm around her and pulled her close.

Brittney felt uncomfortable and wanted to pull away, but she didn't want to upset him. Chase had been a friend to her before they dated and had helped her land many deals with different brands.

"I've been keeping busy!" she said and tried to pull away from him, but his grip was tight.

Chase's eyes were trained on Jasper when he said, "I've missed you," before planting a kiss on her lips.

"Oh, I didn't know you were her boyfriend. Welcome to Willow Heights! I hope you will love it here," Mary Elle said before excusing herself.

Jasper followed behind her without saying a word. He didn't even look at Brittney and that kind of hurt. She didn't want Jasper to see her with Chase and think badly of her. This wasn't who she was. She only befriended and dated guys like Chase because it was what was expected of her. Jasper had seen her for who she was, and she hoped he wouldn't change his mind about her.

"Where are you staying?" Chase asked as he grabbed Brittney's chin and pulled her attention back to him.

"I'm staying at the Inn right on the square."

"Oh, I thought you might be staying here, as most of your posts are about this place. Are they paying you to post about them?"

"No, they're like family, and I genuinely love being here."

"You shouldn't work for free."

"It's not work."

"Are you hungry? I'm starving. Where should we go eat?"

Brittney wasn't sure how she felt about Chase being in town and surprising her. She didn't know if it would be a good idea to have lunch at the restaurant within Willow Acres or if it would be best to go to Main Street.

"I know you raved about the restaurant they have here. I'm sure we can find a nice table inside. What do you think, Brit?" Chase asked as he pulled her toward the pathway that leads to the restaurant.

"I guess we can eat here," Britney said defeatedly.

Once inside the restaurant, Ginger, the waitress, seated them by the big window that looked out to the lake.

"Here are the menus. Can I take your drink order?" Ginger asked with a huge smile as she looked at Chase and noticed he was a fresh face in town.

"We'll have water, thank you," Chase answered with a polite smile.

"I'll be right back with your water," Ginger said as she walked away to give them time to look the menu over.

"So, what brings you here, Chase?" Brittney asked.

"You know, I was worried about you because you had not been very active with your blog or social media postings, and I wanted to make sure you were ok. I worry about you; you know that."

"I'm fine. I just wanted to take some days off and enjoy the moments I've been experiencing here."

"That's good. How is the feature coming along?"

"Good, except I, might lose it because Carol sent a wedding planner without telling me, and she's trying to take over Melanie's wedding. Melanie's not happy about that, understandably so. I don't blame her. It's rude to send someone to re-do your wedding and take away your dream wedding."

"That was messed up. Why would Carol do that?"

"I don't know, but it almost cost me my friendship with Melanie. She's my best friend, and Carol was out of line."

"She asked me about you several times for the same reasons. You've been slacking on your postings and blogs. That's dangerous for your career. You can lose followers and sponsors. You have to be active, even a small post or photo."

"I've just wanted to keep my journey here private. I'll get back to posting senseless things soon and promoting things and places that don't add value to your life. There is so much more to life than just material things."

"Here's your water. Are you ready to place your orders?" Ginger asked as she placed the glasses of water on the coasters, along with some napkins and utensils.

"I'll have a house salad with dressing on the side, please," Brittney said, giving Ginger her menu back.

"I'll have the same, thank you," Chase said as he handed Ginger his menu.

"You've changed a lot since we last spoke," Chase said seriously. He looked at Brittney as if he was trying to figure her out.

"I guess being here has allowed me to think and analyze many aspects of life."

"I hope you understand. This isn't your home. You don't belong here, Brittney. You love the spotlight and the luxury. We all do. How can you be happy living here? They don't even have a movie theater, I'm sure."

"Actually, they do, and they also have a drive-in," Brittney said with a hint of annoyance in her voice.

Brittney began to wonder about the real reason for Chase's visit, but for now, she would observe his every move and let him tell her of his own accord.

"And who is that guy you were hanging around with?"

"He's my good friend, Jasper."

"You like barn animals now?"

"Yes, in fact, I do. I've assisted in helping Jasper deliver a birched calf. It was the most profound and amazing experience I've had so far. I got to witness life and death in a sense."

"Here are the salads you ordered. Would you like some parmesan cheese?" Ginger asked as she held the cheese and the grater.

"Yes, please," they both said at the same time.

"Thank you," Brittney said as she started to eat her salad.

"I never expected you to enjoy being here. I thought these people were paying you to say nice things about the countryside. I just can't believe my eyes."

"I genuinely like this place. My reviews and posts about Willow Acres and Willow Heights are completely honest and true."

"Ok, I'm convinced," Chase said as he shook his head.

"When are you going back to New York?"

"Soon"

"Well, I hope you understand that you are my ex-boyfriend, and you can't mingle with my business."

"Besides the wedding, why are you here, then?"

"Melanie is my best friend. I wanted to help her with the wedding and spend some time relaxing and vacationing."

"I only ask because I care. I got a call from your agent, and she seemed worried about you as well. You weren't posting, and the numbers were going down."

"Yeah, you care about the numbers because that's money coming in or not coming in at all. Besides, I'm working on two different features. I'm not just covering Melanie's wedding. I'm also doing a cute small feature on a new animal sanctuary opening soon. Our readers love animals, and this will also raise awareness and help the sanctuary get more adoptions."

"That is a good topic. Do you need help writing or researching for it?"

"No, thanks. I have it under control. I know the sanctuary owner and have visited them several times."

"Maybe I can go with you next time. I was thinking about adopting a new pet."

"You're never even home, Chase. But sure, you can come with me. I'll be visiting them this afternoon."

"Let's hang out while we wait for the visit."

"You know what? I'll be right back. David, the sanctuary owner, works here during the day. I'll go ask him if we can go now," Brittney said, exasperated by Chase and hoping they could visit now and get this awkward visit from Chase over.

As Brittney walked toward David's office, Jasper crossed paths with her.

"Hey Jasper, have you seen David?"

"I saw him earlier; he was working on some contracts with new vendors for Willow Acres."

"Ok, I wanted to know if I could visit the sanctuary today to take some photos and start writing the feature I was talking to him about. I know that the magazine readers would love to hear his story and get information on the sanc-tuary. Also, Chase, my ex-boyfriend, is interested in adopting a pet from the sanctuary," Brittney said, making sure Jasper understood that Chase was not her boyfriend but rather an ex-boyfriend.

"Maybe he's in his office," Jasper answered coldly.

"Ok, thanks," Brittney said, uncertain about Jasper's answer and not wanting to overanalyze and read too much in-between the lines.

"Knock, knock," Brittney said as she stood in David's office doorway.

"Hey stranger," David said as Brittney walked inside his office and sat at his desk.

"Have you decided on letting me write the feature for the Grand Opening of your sanctuary?"

"Yes, I have, and we agreed to go for it. The grand opening is taking place next weekend. We have already printed flyers and took an ad in the newspaper. We are also including it on the Willow Acres website. It's short notice, but I think it'll work for our town. We spread the news by word of mouth faster than by text or blast emails. We've been working on the barn to make it accessible for everyone and cleared out the dirt road that leads to it."

"Great, that's amazing. I can't wait to see the grand opening. Would it be possible for me to visit today? I have a coworker slash ex-boyfriend that keeps bugging me about visiting your sanctuary," Brittney shared.

"Sure, I don't see why you can't. I'll be leaving work soon because Lindsay is coming over for her monthly check-up. You and your coworker slash ex-boyfriend can come with me," David said with a small smile.

"Thanks, we'll be in the restaurant area. Let me know when you are ready to go."

"Sounds good."

Once Brittney was back at the restaurant and sat down at the table, she told Chase they would visit the sanctuary this afternoon.

"The grand opening is next weekend. They have been advertising it around town, and there's a big hype about it. I hope David gets more animals adopted."

"I'm sure he will. People love animals."

"I appreciate you being here and checking up on me, but I don't like you still acting like we are dating. We've been broken up for several months now. I don't feel comfortable with you putting your arms around me and saying things about us," Brittney said sternly yet politely.

"Ok, I didn't know. I also thought maybe we had a chance to get back together. We've had our ups and downs. I still have strong feelings for you. Why did we break up in the first place?"

"Chase, are you seriously asking me this question?"

"Yes, please tell me. Why did we break up?"

"We broke up because we never saw each other because we were always traveling to different places, and you ended up cheating on me."

"Ok, yeah, but it was just once, and I said I was sorry."

"Chase, please, I don't want to make a scene here, but that's more than enough reasons why we broke up."

"Ok, I guess I was naïve thinking we could be more than friends again."

Brittney rolled her eyes and just shook her head. Why was Chase like this? Before she knew it, she spotted Jasper sitting at the table behind them. He was looking at Brittney with a strange look on his face. Had he just heard their conversation? Brittney was now more mortified by this surprise visit than before. If Jasper had been able to listen to their conversation, at least he would know the truth, that Brittney and Chase were not dating and that she did not want to get back together with him. David texted Brittney a few minutes later to let her know he was heading out to the sanctuary. Brittney and Chase met with David at the parking lot.

"David, this is Chase. He is my coworker and friend."

"Nice to meet you, Chase."

"Likewise," Chase said with a smile.

"Let's head out," David said as he directed them to his truck.

The car ride was pretty quiet. Brittney didn't want to talk to Chase, and Chase was not in a good mood either.

"Here we are," David said as he drove down the dirt road and parked in front of his red barn. It was big, and it was across the new stable David had built for his new horse and a pony coming to the sanctuary soon. David was now trying to rescue horses, donkeys, and ponies headed to the slaughter-house in Mexico. He paid to get them off the trucks and take them to his sanctuary. So far, he could afford the horse and the pony, but he envisioned his stable full of rescue horses that could no longer be used for racing.

"Nice place you have here," Chase said as he looked around.

"Come inside the barn. That's where we have most of our rescued animals," David said proudly.

"Soon, you'll need another barn," Chase said as he petted a goat.

"Or someone can adopt them. They are still good animals."

"The grand opening will help promote the sanctuary and get some adoptions going," Brittney said as she took photos of the animals.

"When is the grand opening?" Chase asked.

"Next weekend," David said as he checked to ensure the animals had water and food.

The grand opening for the sanctuary was here. Thomas and Mary Elle helped set up tables to have guests register for adoptions, volunteering, or sponsorship opportunities. Sienna and Tiffany helped with setting up the snacks and beverage tables. Melanie and Cade helped put up giant balloons to draw people to come down the dirt road and into the sanctuary. Wyatt helped Jasper put the animals in certain areas around the barn for effortless flow and access for the visitors.

Everyone was helping and ready to answer any questions they might have. Brittney arrived with Chase, who was still in town. He said he wanted to see the pony that David had just rescued as he wasn't there when he first visited the sanctuary before.

Many people from Willow Heights and Winding Creek came for the event. Lindsay had also helped David spread the word about the grand opening. She was there with her team of vet techs, ready to give care instructions for any animals that had long-term treatments with her, so the new parents would know how to take care of their newly-adopted animal.

The girls were at the animal sanctuary with Jasper and David taking photos of the magazine feature. It was nice and cool out. David now had three new puppies and a silky chicken with seven little chicks.

"Britt, I think you should just move to Willow Heights," Tiffany said as she brushed Livy's hair.

Livy was a wired-haired dachshund puppy that David rescued. The family that gave her up had found her on the side of the road. The small dog had been terrified of everything, which caused her to act out. She found it especially hard to be around men. Livy had built a bond with Tiffany early on and was starting to warm up to David and Jasper.

"Why?" Brittney asked as she petted a small chick.

"Don't you love it here?" Tiffany asked as if it wasn't obvious.

"I do, but my life is in New York. What would I do here? Where would I work?"

"Isn't the beauty of being an influencer that you can work from anywhere?" Melanie asked.

"Well, yeah. I don't know. It's a huge change."

"I would love to have you here, and I'm sure I'm not the only one," Melanie said with a giggle.

"Have you seen the way he looks at her?" Tiffany asked.

"What are you two talking about?" Brittney asked, confused.

"Jasper, don't pretend you don't know he has a crush on you," Tiffany said, and Melanie nodded in agreement.

"No way. I'm helping him find a girlfriend. He deserves someone better than me, anyway."

"What does that mean?" Melanie asked, sitting up.

"I'm damaged."

"No, you're not," Melanie said.

"Mrs. Adelman always says everyone is searching for love. But when you find someone that doesn't try to change you.

Someone you don't have to explain yourself to. That's when you know you've found the one. I think Jasper might be good for you," Tiffany told her.

"We don't all get a happy ending, you guys. Some of us just need to get by."

"What are you talking about? Where is all of this coming from?" Melanie asked.

"Do you really think I left home because I wanted to be an influencer? I left home because I was tired of fixing my mom. I was a kid! She should've been fixing me. But mom was never the same after dad left us. She hated her job, and most of the time, I felt like she hated me. She never looked for me until she saw me on tv. Then she reached out, but only because she needed money. I'm not a monster, so I send her money every month. But we didn't all grow up with a Mary Elle at home. I've tried reaching out to my mother, but she doesn't want anything to do with me."

"I'm so sorry, Britt. I had no idea."

"It's ok; I never told you any of this. I didn't want to drag you into my drama or for you to feel sorry for me.

"I'm sorry about all this, Britt. I know you're not a monster. I'm sure your mother was going through a lot when your father left, and she didn't know how to cope with it, but it didn't mean she didn't love you. Maybe she felt 'damaged' and unfit to take care of you, and that's why she thought you left her and didn't go looking for you. Either way, we are all just assuming why she did or didn't do things. We don't know her reasons, and you'll never know if you are right or wrong unless you talk to her and ask her," Melanie said.

"I feel ashamed that I've lied to you as well. I wasn't honest, and I wasn't me. I made up this new life for me to be liked and to be someone different. It's been a burden carrying this secret around with me. Now that you know the real me, I hope we can still be friends and that things between us don't change."

"I love you even more now. I didn't know all you went through, Britt; it's not pity. I can't imagine living with a secret like this or feeling unloved by my mother. I know it hasn't been easy for you. I'm here for you in anything you need," Melanie said as she hugged Britney, and Tiffany followed along and hugged her.

By the end of the grand opening, several animals were adopted. David used this event to share information about the horses, donkeys, and ponies auctioned off for the slaughterhouse and taken to Mexico and other countries for their meat. Brittney's social media posts helped David get several sponsors for food and building materials to expand and improve his barn and stable.

Mrs. Adelman and Teddy adopted a little goat. They decided to keep 'Girly' at the Inn as a special guest. Girly had a charming personality.

DeeAnn adopted another cat so that Mittens would not be alone all day. She named him Tom.

Rita and Bob fell in love with new puppies but only adopted one. They named him Duke. They hoped Penny would accept him and it would bring her some companionship, especially now that Rita and Sienna would have to spend more time at the boutique.

Melanie and Cade contemplated getting a puppy from the two left but weren't sure if Goldie, the kitten Cade, had given Melanie when he proposed, would like the new puppy. As they discussed this with Lindsay, she told them it would be the best time to introduce a puppy to her household since Goldie was still a kitten. They would grow up together and not see each other as rivals. Melanie and Cade adopted the puppy and named him Lucky.

Jasper had his eye on the last puppy and decided to adopt

him and name him Dimka. He would train him to help him at work and when he came to help David.

The event was a huge success, and many people signed up to volunteer. There was now more space in the barn for new animals to be rescued. Chase did not adopt any animals, but he was also busy posting on all his social media accounts about the sanctuary, and he, too, was able to get a few sponsorships for David. All in all, it was a great blessing to have this feature in the animal sanctuary.

* * *

BEING in Willow Heights almost felt like being back home for Brittney. Maybe it was the small-town feel or just seeing Mary Elle with her daughters. Brittney had tried to ignore it for a long time, but she missed her mom. After the emotional conversation she had with Melanie and Tiffany, Brittney called her mother. It had been two days since she called and left a message, but her mother never called back. She also sent her a message online, and it showed that it had been read, but she never replied.

She was now sitting at the overlook, and she wondered what she could do to make things right. The rain was coming down, but she didn't care. She let it fall on her; at least it hid the tears coming down her face. She got herself out again and saw that her mother was online. She was about to message her again when lightning struck.

She grabbed her things and began to run for shelter. She would never be able to reconcile with her mother if she got struck by lightning.

"Britt, come here!" she heard someone call out.

She turned to see where the voice was coming from, but it was hard to see with the rain coming down hard. An ATV appeared next to her, and Jasper said something she couldn't hear. She jumped in with him, and they took off to the barn. Once inside the barn, Jasper offered her a dry t-shirt.

"What were you doing out there?" he asked.

"I just wanted to be alone."

"Is everything okay? Is there anything you want to talk about?"

"No, I'm fine. How was your date?"

"It was fine," Jasper said and rushed off.

"Fine? That's all you have to say?"

"What do you want me to say?"

"I don't know. Anything. Did you like her? Would you go on a second date with her?"

"No," he said.

"No? Just, no?" Tiffany asked, confused.

She'd seen the pictures; Beth was beautiful. What guy wouldn't like her?

"Yes, just no."

"Why not?"

Jasper rolled his eyes and left out a long sigh.

"Britt, do you really not know? Or do you just want to pretend you don't because you don't think I'm good enough?"

"What are you talking about?"

"I don't like Beth, just like I didn't like the last girl, and I won't like the next girl. Because they're not you."

"Those girls are much better matches for you than me."

"Why? Because I don't drive a BMW? Because I don't travel or have a lot of money?"

"No. How can you say that? Jasper, you deserve someone better than me," Brittney said and quickly left. She didn't care if she got soaked again. She needed to get away. Brittney jumped into the driver's seat of her rented car and went to the inn. She didn't stop to make small talk with Mrs. Adelman like she usually did. She just wanted to be alone.

She hated that Jasper felt that he wasn't good enough for her when it was the complete opposite. Britney didn't see herself the way others did. She didn't see the good in herself and all she had to offer. She felt broken and like she couldn't deserve someone loving or nice. She had convinced herself that no one else could ever love and understand her apart from her grandmother. She missed her grandmother dearly, and when she was in a dark place like now, she would often speak out loud to herself and pretend like her grandmother could hear her and was there to help her through.

"Grandma, I don't know what to do. I've tried reaching out to her, but it seems like she's not interested in me," Brittney said, almost whispering as her tears rolled down her face.

In silence in her room at the Inn, Brittney took out her journal and wrote how she felt and missed her grandmother. Suddenly, a notification said she had just received a message. As Brittney looked at the app, she discovered it was from her mother, and it read: 'Hello Brittney' with a smiley face. She couldn't believe it; it was as if God had heard her conversation with her grandmother and decided to intervene.

Brittney quickly replied, "It's good to hear from you. How are you?"

They exchanged pleasantries, and Brittney began to tell her mom how she was feeling, and soon they were able to video chat.

"I'm sorry it took me so long to realize what a horrible mother I have been to you, Brittney."

"It's ok, mom. I never talked to you about how I was feeling. Instead, I ran away from my feelings and you. I didn't know how to deal with losing grandma. I know you were going through a lot dealing with dad leaving us and picking up the pieces."

"I know that I could have tried to be a better mother. I

could have gone after you when you left, but I felt that maybe you would be happier away from me. I was in shambles when your dad left. I drank a lot, and I was in a dark place. I functioned as best as I could. I neglected you. I'm so sorry."

"We all make mistakes; you didn't know how to deal with your pain and your new responsibilities as a single parent. I just wanted to tell you how I've been feeling all this time and why I left. I want to fix our relationship."

"I would love that. I know that when I came back to your life, I was still dealing with things and trying to get my life in order, and that's why I asked if you could help me out financially. You must have thought that I was taking advantage of you. But I don't care about money; I can see that I've needed you and a mother-daughter relationship. You're all I have left in this life, Brittney."

"I'm visiting my friend Melanie in Georgia. I don't know if you would like to come to her wedding as my plus one."

"I would love that. I have a new job, but I will ask for the days off. Email me the dates, please."

"I will, and I'll get you the airplane ticket and anything else you need. I'm so excited to start reconnecting with you, mom."

"Me too. I'm blessed to have such an amazing and forgiving daughter as you. I don't deserve your love and forgiveness."

"I'm the one that has to be forgiven."

"I know I haven't said this enough, but I love you, Brittney."

It was almost like a dream come true for Brittney. She couldn't believe that her mother had reached out to her and that they spoke on the phone and through text messages for hours. Brittney expressed herself and heard from her mother directly what happened and why things happened the way they did. She felt a renewed hope that things between them would improve and that maybe she would get her happy ending.

Brittney couldn't wait to tell Melanie and Tiffany about her texts and phone call with her mother and how she would be coming for her wedding. It was all she could think about. That night Brittney was so thrilled she couldn't even fall asleep. She was already thinking about outfits and gifts she would have ready for her mom. She was also planning on asking Mrs. Adelman if there was a suite at the Inn for her mom to stay in to put her gifts and flowers before her arrival. It felt like Christmas had come early for her. That night before she finally closed her eyes and fell asleep, she thanked God for listening to her request and for answering her so quickly.

CHAPTER 12

"Good morning, Mom. Ready for Ryder?" Melanie asked as she took Ryder out of his stroller and walked into Mary Elle's office.

"I'm always ready for my Ryder," Mary Elle said as she took her grandson from Melanie.

"Thanks for helping me with him tonight. It feels like now that Cade and I are engaged with a wedding right around the corner, we don't see each other at all," Melanie said, pouting.

"I know, you have to enjoy your time together now. Make sure to always have at least one night a week for date night. Trust me, don't let work or the kids get in the way of romance after marriage."

"Thanks for the advice. You're right. I'll add that to my vows, too," Melanie said with a wide smile, knowing that Mary Elle was sharing knowledge.

"Have your bridesmaids tried on their dresses for the last fitting?"

"Yes, Sienna is finally back in town. She's staying here for two months, and Rita is over the moon. They have been working so hard on opening their boutique. I already have something in mind for Ryder when he gets older."

"I know, I've been meaning to go down to Main Street and help them, but I've been so busy with so many weddings and Wyatt and life," Mary Elle said, wishing she had more hours in a day.

"How is Wyatt? Have you spoken to Molly about the breakup?"

"No, I don't want to ask her why she left my sweet boy with a broken heart. I don't want to get too involved. She's also a co-worker, and I want to respect their privacy."

"Yeah, I know. Have you spoken with Wyatt?"

"He's been all gloomy. It breaks my heart. He feels rejected yet again by someone he loved. He's such a great kid; why can't people see that?"

"I'm sure they see it, but they just can't appreciate it, or maybe they were just passing through his life. Maybe Molly wasn't the right girl for him. We have to keep the faith and know that God will heal all his wounds."

"You're right. On a positive note, he's spending more time playing basketball, and he's gotten better. Even Thomas is playing basketball again. There's always a blessing hidden within every situation. Thanks for reminding me of that, Mel," Mary Elle said.

* * *

MELANIE INVITED ANN, Cade's stepmother, and his sister Alana over to her place to help with the wedding favors. She hoped that this would help them bond. Melanie had spent the whole day cleaning and cooking. She wanted to make the very best impression on them. She knew the importance of having the family's support, and she liked that more than anything.

"You missed a spot," Tiffany said as Melanie vacuumed the house for the third time this afternoon.

"Where?" Melanie asked as she looked for the spot.

"She's kidding," Sienna said as she threw a cushion at Tiffany. Tiffany giggled, and Melanie rolled her eyes.

"I want to make a good impression on them. This day means a lot to me," Melanie told them.

"I know, Mel. Ann isn't going to decide you're not a good match for Cade because you overcooked the chicken or because there's dust on your mantle."

"What?" Melanie asked with a horrified look.

"You're an amazing girl, and I'm sure they see that."

"You think I overcooked the chicken?" Melanie asked as she grabbed a microfiber cloth and wiped the mantle.

Tiffany looked at Sienna for support.

"What Tiffany is saying is that you need to calm down. Today will be great, and you and Cade will have a beautiful life together," Sienna said.

"They're here!" Tiffany said as they heard a car door shut outside.

"How do I look? Is there anything in my teeth? Is my hair frizzy?" Melanie asked.

"You're picture-perfect," Sienna assured her.

"Welcome!" Tiffany said as she let Ann and Alana in.

"Thank you for having us," Ann said.

"Melanie!" Alana said as she hugged her soon-to-be sister-in-law.

"Hi, welcome to my little house," Melanie said.

"Ann, do you know Melanie was the one that talked some sense into me when I was going to marry Matty?"

"Did she?" Ann asked with a look that Melanie couldn't read.

Melanie remembered talking to Alana about her engagement and how torn Alana had been. Matt was one of Cade's best friends and a very nice guy, but Alana hadn't felt like she was really in love with him. Melanie hadn't known how Cade's family felt about Alana's engagement. What if they liked Matt? What if they were rooting for their relationship?

"If Matt and I would've gotten married, he never would've met Sandy. He is so much happier now."

"He sure is," Ann said.

"So, why don't you guys come over to the dining table? We have everything ready here," Tiffany said.

Melanie gave her sister a grateful smile, and Tiffany gave her a wink.

"Oh, I am Melanie's sister, and this is our cousin, Sienna," Tiffany told them as they took their seats.

"Pleased to meet you both," Ann said.

"It's great meeting you two as well," Sienna said as she grabbed a couple of shopping bags and began to pull things out, "So, we got disposable cameras, which we will cover with these custom decals that we ordered online."

The custom decals for the disposable cameras read: 'Help us capture our big day' and instructed the guests to capture all the heartwarming, funny, and sweet moments on their wedding day.

"As you all know, Cade is huge on music, and he made a mix of the wedding playlist. We have the CDs here and need to adhere to the custom stickers," Tiffany said.

The custom stickers had the wedding playlists and a special sweet message from Cade to Melanie.

"Lastly, we have sparklers that we need to prepare," Melanie said as she showed them the sparklers and the ribbon they would be tied around them. The ribbon read, 'let love sparkle' with the couple's name and wedding date.

They quickly got to work, and Melanie began to relax. Everyone was getting along, and she got to know the two most influential women in Cade's life. Ann asked if she could speak to Melanie in private as they began wrapping up.

Melanie took Ann to her bedroom, where they could speak privately.

"I know you're nervous, and you want to make a good impression on us," Ann said.

"I am. You do not know how badly I want you guys to approve of me."

"We do. We love you!"

"You do?"

"Yes, I've never seen Cade happier than he is now. I've seen how you treat him and how you look at him, and that's love. True love," Ann said as she covered Melanie's hand with hers.

"I love him, and I promise to be the best wife to him."

"I know you will be, sweetheart. I brought something for you," Ann said as she pulled a necklace out of her jacket pocket. "This necklace belonged to Cade's mother. She gave it to me before she passed away, and I would like to give it to you. John gave it to her after Cade was born," Ann explained as she motioned for Melanie to turn so she could put it on her. The necklace was a heart locket with Cade's name and date of birth.

"Thank you," Melanie said as she gently touched the necklace.

"She would've wanted you to have it," Ann said as she hugged Melanie. "Please know that John and I couldn't be happier to have you in our family."

"I'm honored to be a part of your family. Thank you so much," Melanie said with happy tears in her eyes.

CHAPTER 13

Melanie's bridal shower and Cade's bachelor party would be combined into one big event. Everyone was excited to see what they would plan. Cade and Melanie had decided to share this special event with friends and family and with each other. They had talked about having a cool camping trip or having a big barbecue but decided that it would be in Mary Elle's house by the lake. There they would be able to fish, have a barbecue, have some competitive games, and go for a swim in the lake.

"Tiffany, you and mom outdid yourselves with this party!" Melanie said as she and Cade walked hand in hand to her mother's house, where Sienna and Brittney greeted them.

They were handed some sunglasses with 'Cade & Melanie's Bridal Party' on either side of the glasses frame. As they walked further inside the house, they were greeted by David and Wyatt, who handed them white caps that read 'Bride to be' and "Groom to be.' Several picnic tables with cute tablecloths in white, light peach, and pink. Thomas was already barbecuing some chicken breast, meat and vegetable skewers, and hot dogs. There was also a table with ice buckets, beers, wine coolers, water, and soda. Under a canopy, there were tables with fun little cupcakes, a vintage popcorn machine, cotton candy machine, strawberry goat cheese bruschetta, Caprese appetizer, mini southern pimento cheese cups, mini layered Waldorf salads, guacamole and chips, mini quiches, chocolate-covered strawberries, heart-shaped donuts with pink glaze, yogurt parfait bar including honey for drizzling. Everything was perfect and fun.

"Cade, let's go to the lake and fish," David said while handing Cade the fishing rod and tackle box.

"Let's go," Cade said as he gave Melanie a tender kiss on the lips before heading off with David, Wyatt, and Bill.

"Bye, have fun, see you soon," Melanie said as she waved him bye.

"Don't look so sad. He's just at the lake! We are going swimming soon," Tiffany said as she noticed that Melanie's smile had faded a little.

"I know," Melanie said as she fixed Ryder's little swimming diaper and put some sunscreen lotion on him and a cute floppy little hat.

"Here's a little floatie I got for him," Sienna said as they walked toward the lake.

"Aw, that's so cute. Thank you," Melanie replied.

"I hope you're enjoying your party."

"I am. It's always nice to be around friends and family."

"Did you decide where you'll be going for the honeymoon yet?"

"Yeah, we finally decided on Sedona. We love hiking, and we found a cool cabin out in the desert near a canyon. We are excited. I'm so grateful that you, Tiffany, and Britney will be helping me with Ryder. I didn't want to overwhelm my mom with him. She's already worked so hard to plan this party, the wedding, and working."

"It's no problem. I love being around Ryder. He always

makes me smile. I ran into Dr. Banks the other day while Rita and I were signing off the lease for the office on Main Street for the boutique, and she offered me a job. I haven't told Rita or Bob yet, but I wanted to tell you. You've become one of my best friends ever since I came looking for Rita."

"That's amazing! Are you going to take the job here?"

"Yes, I think I am. We are just working out a contract, but I have a really good feeling about it. I'm excited. God has answered all my prayers. I'm just happy about life. I've never really been happy before, not like this, but everything's coming together and taking place now."

"That's wonderful. I'm so happy for you," Melanie said as she gave Sienna a side hug.

As Melanie and Sienna were about to head to the lake, she caught a glimpse of red hair.

"Ruby?" Melanie asked.

"It's me!" Ruby said as she walked into the room.

"I thought you said you couldn't make it! I'm so happy you're here," Melanie said as she hugged her childhood friend.

"I wouldn't miss this for the world. Not sure if you remember me, but hi!" Ruby said as she hugged Sienna as well.

"Of course, I remember you," Sienna said with a chuckle as she returned the hug.

"Can you believe you're getting married? Remember all the times we had to pretend weddings in our backyards growing up?"

"Yes, I remember we always made Tiffany be the groom," Melanie said with a giggle.

"Where is Tiff?" Ruby asked as she glanced around and didn't spot her.

"She's by the lake. We were just heading back there now."

"Okay, I'll meet you guys there in a little bit. I want to talk to Mary Elle and Rita first."

"Sure, see you there!" Melanie said as she and Sienna went back to the lake.

"What took you girls so long?" Tiffany said she had gone ahead of them to find a good spot and lay out their beach towels and some toys for Ryder.

"We changed Ryder," Melanie answered. The weather was perfect. It was not too chilly or hot yet. It was mid-Spring, and it was just gorgeous weather. The sky was clear, and the sun was just right.

"What an adorable floatie. It's like a chair," Tiffany said as she examined the float.

"Sienna got it for Ryder."

"Cool. Are you thirsty or hungry, Mel?" Tiffany asked as she headed back to the house to grab some finger food and drinks.

"Sure, I could eat some Caprese appetizers and have a soda."

"I'll go with you, Tiff," Sienna said as she ran after Tiffany.

Melanie sat and played with Ryder while she waited for the girls to come back. Soon after, more guests arrived and enjoyed the lake as they swam and fished.

"It's game time," Mary Elle announced and gathered everyone to go back to the backyard to participate.

"Ok, who's ready for the first game?" Sienna said as the guests took their seats at the picnic tables.

"The first game is 'Who Knows the Couple Best.' Please write down your answers with the pencil provided at each table," Mary Elle said. Each contestant got a sheet of paper where they were asked multiple questions. They had to select the correct answer. The questions asked how they met, where their first date was, who said I love you first, and how Cade proposed, among many other questions. Tiffany and

David kept playfully bantering with each other. In the end, they both tied, but the winner of this game was Jasper. He received a cool portable waterproof Bluetooth speaker.

"The next game is 'The Shoe Game,'" Sienna said as Tiffany handed out the following cards. This game was similar to the last, but the questions were focused on each individual. Some of the questions asked were what month was the bride born? What is the groom's eye color? Is the bride a morning or night person? How many siblings does the bride have? What is the groom's favorite genre of music? The winner of this fun game was Wyatt. He won a cool cell-phone case.

"Ok, folks, the next game is the 'Tie the Knot relay. Each couple ties their ankles together, collects the items needed to plant their flowers, and brings them back to the table where the relay began. They need to place the plants, flowers, pots, shovels, and gloves. The winners of this game were Bill and Barbara. They won a brunch at Willow Acre's restaurant.

Everyone was having such a great time; it was a lovely afternoon. After the games, everyone sat down and enjoyed hot dogs, grilled or barbecued chicken, and grilled fish. The sunset was beautiful, there was music and dancing, and everyone was laughing and having a great time. The love was evident, and Melanie couldn't help but be grateful that this was her life now. For a long time, she thought she would be stuck in an unhappy marriage with a man that strongly disliked her family; but here she was with Cade, who loved her and her family and her son. Cade looked over at her and squeezed her hand before bringing it to his lips and planting a kiss on it.

"I love you," he whispered in her ear.

"I love you more."

* * *

THE REHEARSAL DINNER was set for the night before the wedding. Melanie's nerves were already on edge, and she was trying to control the Bridezilla inside her. She was trying to stay out of everyone's way. She wasn't going to be controlling. Melanie would trust her mom and her abilities. She was grateful that everyone arrived at Mary Elle's house on time. The seats were already set out, the tables to sign the wedding book was out by the front, and the crew was still working on setting up the altar. Melanie looked at Cade and knew that no matter what could go wrong tomorrow during their big day, it would not affect their love for each other or take away from their special day.

"Good evening, John and Ann," Mary Elle said as she greeted Cade's parents. Alana, his sister, was running a little late for the rehearsal dinner.

"Thank you, Mary Elle. Your home is beautiful as always," Ann said as they walked in and were directed to the dining room.

"Mr. and Mrs. Thorne, so glad you made it," Melanie said as she walked over to them with Cade and Ryder.

"We wouldn't miss this important night," John said as he gave Cade's shoulder a friendly squeeze and offered to carry Ryder.

"Alana is running late," Ann explained.

"She texted us. I hope she gets here soon," Melanie said with a smile.

As soon as everyone arrived, they began rehearsing. Each bridesmaid and groomsman took their place in line and walked down the aisle as the DJ played the song. Then they stood at the altar, which was now finished. Then the flower girl did her part, the ring bearer, the groom's parents, and Thomas and Mary Elle. Barbara will walk down with Michael, but Wyatt will take his place instead since he wasn't there yet. They hoped Michael and Samantha would be on time tomorrow for the actual wedding. Michael couldn't arrive earlier because of conflicting flight schedules for work. Finally, Melanie and Bill rehearsed their walk down the aisle. It was all feeling so real. Melanie's nerves were on edge, but she felt a sense of peace come over her when her eyes met Cade's. She knew this was the best decision and the biggest blessing in her life. There was nothing to fear, and things would be great this time because they both loved each other and wanted the same things in life. They had discussed all these things and had agreed on everything. There would be no surprises to any of them. After rehearsing, dinner was ready.

Dinner was amazing. Mary Elle's famous home cooked crispy andouille hush puppies, shrimp and grits, fried green tomatoes, pan-fried chicken, Ceasar salad, buttermilk biscuits, sweet tea, and banana pudding. Everyone ate until they couldn't eat anymore. A few buttons had to be undone, but it was all worth it.

CHAPTER 14

After the debacle of not having a cake for the wedding and getting rid of Carol and Claire, the wedding was finally here. Melanie was nervous and excited to walk down the aisle and say 'I do' to her best friend.

"Everyone's here," Mary Elle said as she walked into the room where Melanie was getting ready.

"Did Michael and Samantha make it yet?" Melanie asked as Sienna fixed her veil and helped her get up to walk towards the door.

"They're not here yet, but they are on their way. The flight was delayed. Your father is with Cade and Wyatt in his room, getting ready. Thomas had misplaced Cade's cufflinks, but they had been in his pocket all along. Tiffany and Britney have Ryder. They're working on the finishing touches and showing everyone to their seats." Mary Elle updated Melanie on everyone's whereabouts. Melanie had been a little Bridezilla during the rehearsal; therefore, Mary Elle expected her questions and concerns like any great wedding planner would.

"Is Rita here?" Melanie asked.

"Yes, she's here and is waiting to come see you. Are you ready for her?"

"Yes, I am," Melanie said.

"I'll go get her."

"Mom loves you so much," Sienna told Melanie once they were alone.

"You called her mom," Melanie said as she got teary-eyed. She was highly emotional today.

"Yes, I've only said it to you for now. I know I should call them mom and dad, but I'm taking baby steps. I don't want to step on anyone's toes."

Melanie understood where Sienna was coming from. Things had gotten a little complicated when the rest of the kids found out about Sienna. Alexander, Rita, and Bob had raised him and his siblings after Rita's sister couldn't have them anymore.

"Have you told them the good news?"

"No, not yet. I haven't had the chance yet. After I told you, Dr. Banks confirmed it yesterday," Sienna responded with a huge smile.

"This is what Rita and Bob have been praying for all this time," Melanie said as Rita walked into the room.

"Melanie, you look breathtaking. I am so happy for you. This is a blessing from God." Rita said as she hugged Melanie and extended her left arm to include Sienna.

"I'm blessed to have you and Bob in my life, aunt Rita," Melanie said with tears filling in her eyes.

"Don't cry, dear. Today is a day of love and happiness. I wanted to see you and give you this," Rita said as she handed Melanie a small box.

"What is it?" Melanie asked as she slowly opened it.

Rita and Sienna exchanged nervous smiles. They had worked so hard on it and hoped that Melanie would like it. It was a sapphire butterfly hairpin.

"Oh my, it's beautiful. Did you make this for me?"

"Yes, Sienna and I worked on it and made it with all our love. I hope you love it and will wear it today."

"I will; it's gorgeous. I was missing something blue for today. This is perfect."

Rita helped Sienna place it in Melanie's hair, and it looked amazing. It was truly perfect and the finishing touch that brought everything together.

"There's someone here who wants to see you," Mary Elle said as she peeked inside the room. She stepped inside the room, and Bill walked in behind her.

"We'll give you some privacy," Mary Elle said as Rita and Sienna followed her.

"You're stunning, sweetheart," Bill said with proud tears.

"I'm so happy you're here, dad," Melanie said as she hugged him.

"I wouldn't miss this for the world. I am so proud of the woman that you are. You're an amazing mother, and I do not doubt that you will be a great wife to Cade. He is one lucky guy."

"Thank you, dad."

"You and your siblings are my greatest achievements. Being your father is the greatest honor. I couldn't be prouder of you all. I got you a small gift," he said as he pulled out a small, long box.

Tiffany opened it and let out a small gasp, "It's gorgeous, dad."

"Let me put it on you," he said as he took the tennis bracelet out of the box and placed it around her small wrist.

"I love it, dad. Thank you!" Melanie said as she hugged her dad.

"Only the best for my baby girl," he said.

A light knock was followed by Mary Elle saying it was almost time.

"I'll let you finish getting ready. I love you, Mel."

"I love you, dad," she said before giving him another hug.

Her relationship with her father had been a rocky one. He had never been around much as they were growing up. When she found out her father had been unfaithful, it truly broke her heart. She had always thought their parents had a perfect marriage. She thought they were in love with each other. Sure, they didn't go on family vacations, and her father was always at work, but she thought that was just how things were with grownups. Things were much better now. Bill was actively trying to be a part of their life, and he had shown how remorseful he was about his past actions. There was no point in being stuck in the past. Life was too short.

Shortly after Bill walked out, Mary Elle, Rita, and Sienna came back inside. Mary Elle freshened Melanie's makeup and wiped away the smudges created during her interaction with her father.

"It's time, my sweet girl," Mary Elle said with tears in her eyes.

"Don't cry, mom. I will ruin my makeup again," Melanie said, fanning her face.

"I'm just so happy," Mary Elle said as she smoothed Melanie's hair.

"I love you, mom. Thank you for planning my wedding. Thank you for always being there. You're the best, and I can't imagine my life without you."

"Oh, Melanie!" Mary Elle said as she pulled her into a hug and tried to keep herself from crying.

"I'll go ahead of you to find my seat next to Bob and the kids," Rita said as she walked out of the room.

"Let's go," Melanie said as she walked with Sienna, holding her dress train.

"Cade and the groomsmen are at the altar. Bill is ready for you; here he comes," Mary Elle whispered.

Melanie gave her mom one last hug before meeting her father.

* * *

MELANIE AND BILL stood on the deck behind Mary Elles' house, looking toward the altar, where she saw Cade standing and smiling at her. She felt the millions of butterflies in her stomach swirling inside, and she took a deep breath and looked at Bill, who was crying tears of joy. The moment their eyes met, Cade broke out into the biggest smile she'd ever seen on his handsome face. All the nerves in her stomach settled. That was going to be her husband. The man that always made her feel safe and loved. She couldn't wait to spend forever with him.

As the music procession began, Melanie and Bill walked down the aisle. Melanie was breathtaking, and she looked so in love. She was wearing a form-fitted beaded white maxi dress with off-the-shoulder straps. Cade was handsome as always in a white suit. He had not stopped smiling since he saw her at the end of the aisle. Melanie walked down the aisle, looking at Cade the whole time. His love for her was evident in his eyes. She would never take his love for granted. Once they reached the alter, Cade took her hands in his.

"You're breathtaking," Cade whispered.

"Thank you," she whispered back.

"Dearly beloved, we are gathered together here in the sight of God and in the face of this company of witnesses to join together this man and this woman in Holy Matrimony..." Pastor Miller began.

Melanie couldn't stop thinking about how far she'd come as the pastor spoke. She had endured so much pain and heartache in her lifetime, but the moment she let Cade's love in, all the pain and hurt had been washed away. He loved her with the purest love she'd ever experienced.

The ceremony was nothing short of perfect and beautiful. Baby Ryder was there to help his mom and dad light the unity candle that symbolized how they are now one, including Ryder. They were now one big, happy family.

Mary Elle and Tiffany couldn't help but shed tears of joy. What a beautiful love story they had all witnessed.

"I now pronounce you husband and wife. You may kiss the bride," Pastor Miller said as the crowd cheered them on. The happy couple had their first kiss as husband and wife without hesitation. When they pulled apart, Melanie was filled with excitement for the beginning of their life together.

* * *

"You're a sight to behold, Mrs. Thorne," Cade told Melanie as they waited to make their entrance together. While the wedding had taken place at Mary Elle's, the reception would be in Willow Acres.

"Why, thank you, Mr. Thorne," Melanie said as she planted a kiss on his lips.

"I can't believe this day has finally come," Cade said as he pulled Melanie close.

"I know," Melanie said as she gave her husband another kiss.

Mary Elle hired drivers to transport the guests to Willow Acres. The drive wasn't very long, but she wanted everything to go as smoothly as possible. Everything was ready, and the guests took their seats. Mary Elle asked Cade and Melanie to make their way. They walked in hand in hand, waving at everyone. Cade guided Melanie to the dance floor, where they shared their first dance. For their first dance, the song they chose was 'Someone like you by Van Morrison.

"You're everything I've ever wanted, Mel," Cade said as he slowly guided their bodies around the dance floor.

When their song ended, Bill stepped in and began his dance with Melanie. The song he chose was a ballad version of 'Forever Young' by Rod Stewart. As they danced, he quietly sang it to Melanie.

"I remember listening to this song in the mornings on my way to work when you all were little," Bill said. "This song never fails to make me think of you and your siblings."

"I had no idea, dad. Thank you for sharing that with me."

"I love you so much," Bill said as tears formed in his eyes.

"We love you, Dad," Melanie said as she rested her head on his chest.

When that song ended, 'Blessed' by Thomas Rhett began to play, and everyone joined in on the dance floor.

"May I have this dance?" Thomas asked as he stepped in.

"Of course," Melanie said as her father handed her to Thomas.

"Cade's mother must be smiling from ear to ear up above right now. You're everything she would've wanted for her son."

"Do you think so?" Melanie asked with tears in her eyes.

"Yes, she was a lovely woman. A lot like you."

As the night progressed and a few more songs were danced to before everyone was told to take a seat for the food to be served.

Cade and Melanie took a seat at their table, located at the front of the room. Cade's father and stepmother came over to congratulate them. Mr. Thorne was holding Ryder when they approached.

"Mr. And Mrs. Thorne," Cade's dad, John, said with a wink. Cade stood and hugged his father.

"Welcome to the family, Melanie," Ann said.

"Thank you," Melanie said.

"Ann and I wanted to wish you all the best in your marriage. Melanie, I cannot imagine a better match for my son. Cade, I hope you know God has entrusted you with Melanie and Ryder. May you always honor and care for your family."

"Yes, sir," Cade said as he found Melanie's hand and squeezed it.

CHAPTER 15

Bob, Rita, and their kids had one table right across from Mary Elle, Thomas, Bill, Barbara, Michael, and Samantha. Tiffany and David went over to greet Michael and Samantha. Their flight had been delayed, and they hadn't seen them before. The two happy couples were happily chatting when Bill came over.

"Michael, you made it," Bill said as he approached their table with Barbara.

"Hey, dad," Michael said as Samantha stood next to him.

"I'm so glad to see you. I've missed you, son." Bill said as he hugged Michael.

"Dad, there's someone I would like you to meet," Michael said as he pulled Samantha close to him and said, "this is Samantha, my fiancée."

"Hi, Bill. It's been a while," Samantha said.

Bill was speechless, and his face was paperwhite. His body swayed, and he held on to the back of a seat for support.

"Dad, are you okay?" Tiffany asked as she moved close to her dad and placed a hand on his back.

"What?" Bill said.

"Dad, are you ok?" Michael asked as well.

Bill wasn't looking too good and was clutching his left arm.

"You are engaged to her?" Bill asked as he clung to the back of the seat before sliding down to the floor.

"Dad!" Michael and Tiffany yelled simultaneously.

Tiffany looked at Samantha and was appalled to see her standing next to Michael with a look of satisfaction on her face. It seemed like she had intended to get this reaction from Bill.

"What just happened?" Tiffany asked her, but Samantha didn't answer her.

Cade and Thomas rushed over to see what was going on. David was on the phone, calling for help. After the ambulance and emergency medical services arrived, Samantha was nowhere to be found. Tiffany didn't understand why Bill had this reaction and why Samantha had just disappeared. What was going on?

* * *

"Honey, you shouldn't be here. It's your wedding night. We'll keep you updated," Mary Elle told Melanie as they all waited around in the waiting room of the Winding Creek hospital.

"He's my dad. I have to be here for him. I need to know what's going on. Unless I'm right here, I won't feel good about this. I'll leave as soon as I know he's okay. Our flight doesn't go out till tomorrow afternoon."

Melanie and Cade were flying to Sedona, Arizona, for their honeymoon. Tiffany and Brittney had volunteered to watch Ryder while they were gone. Melanie had been hesitant at first, but after talking with Mary Elle, she agreed to go on her honeymoon without Ryder.

Barbara walked into the waiting room, and everyone turned to her.

"Is he okay?" Mary Elle asked.

"The doctor says he will be fine. He just needs some time to recover. He had a ministroke."

The tension in the room seemed to dwindle. Everyone had been on edge, unsure of what had occurred.

"I think I should clear some things up that might shed some clarity on this situation," Barbara said as she motioned for everyone to take a seat.

"What is it, Barb? Is he okay?"

"Yes, he will be okay. As long as you all find it in your hearts to forgive him."

"Forgive him for what?" Melanie asked as she wiped tears off her face. Cade put a comforting arm around her.

"Tonight was not Bill's first time meeting Samantha. We have reason to believe that she was using Michael to hurt him. During his marriage to you, Mary Elle, Bill stepped out of line a few times. You might only know about the time he was unfaithful with me, but I know of at least two more times."

Mary Elle thought she had come to terms with Bill's unfaithfulness. She had truly forgiven him and moved on, but hearing that he had been unfaithful multiple times throughout her marriage reopened many of those old wounds. Had Bill ever loved her? Had she ever been enough for him? How in the world had she not known?

"So, you're saying my dad was unfaithful with Samantha, and she was using Michael? What for?" Melanie asked. Mary Elle could tell Melanie was trying to control herself, and she was trying not to shout, but she was distraught, and this was not how her wedding night should be going.

"This is bull!" Michael said and abruptly walked out of the waiting room. Mary Elle wanted to go after him, but she couldn't find the strength to stand. Thomas and Cade went after Michael, and the room began to spin. How did such a beautiful night turn out this way?

"Why did Samantha go after Michael?" Tiffany asked.

"When Bill left Mary Elle, Samantha expected him to pick her up. She had been seeing him for many years before he started seeing me. She wanted to tell everyone about their affair, but Bill begged her not to. He thought you already hated him because of his affair with me. He couldn't handle you all finding out about the others. So, he paid her, but I guess that wasn't enough for her."

"This is unbelievable," Mary Elle said.

"Bill isn't a perfect person. But he's trying. He's changed whether you believe it or not. The divorce was a wake-up call for him. You have no idea how many nights he went to sleep crying. He's righting his wrongs. Cast all the stones you want, but tell me, which one of you in here is perfect?"

"None of us are perfect, and we don't pretend to be. But we don't hurt those that we care about. We don't lead double lives, Barb." Tiffany said before she stormed out of the room with David close behind.

"Can I see, Bill?" Mary Elle asked Barbara.

"Yes, he requested to speak to you."

Mary Elle wasn't sure what she would say to Bill. She didn't feel angry, and it wasn't the same feeling of betrayal that she'd felt when he left her for Barabara. She couldn't explain what she was feeling. As she walked into the hospital room and saw Bill lying in the hospital bed surrounded by all the hospital equipment and beeping machines, things became clear for her. She had no choice but to forgive him. She would not let her heart be filled with hate.

"How are you doing?" Mary Elle asked as she stood next to his hospital bed.

"I'm hanging in there. I'm so sorry, Mary Elle," he says as he begins to cry.

"It's in the past, Bill. Let's focus on you getting better," she tells him as she awkwardly pats his hand. Mary Elle really didn't know what else to say. She'd moved on from that, and she is now in a happy marriage. It was a shock to hear it at first, but seeing Bill here now, she knows what's always remained true is that their kids come first. She needs to be strong. He is their father, and he always will be no matter what mistakes he's made. They need him in their life.

"I never did deserve you, Mary Elle. When we were together, I wish I had done things differently. I wish I could've read your mind."

Mary Elle wanted to ask him why he'd done what he'd done. Why had their family never been enough for him? When did he start being unfaithful? But she didn't ask because it wasn't worth going down that path.

"Ellie, do you think they'll ever forgive me?" Bill asked, breaking Mary Elle free from her thoughts.

Mary Elle flinched at the sound of her old nickname. She still hated hearing him call her that. She took a deep breath and carefully thought about what she should say.

"Of course, they will. You're their father, and no matter what, they'll always love you."

"I don't know if Michael will ever forgive me."

"You did not know that Samantha would do that. You can't blame yourself for her actions. She acted on her own. Get some rest, Bill. Focus on getting better, and when you're out from here, you'll be able to work on your relationship with the kids."

"Thank you, Mary Elle. The kids are so lucky to have you."

Mary Elle leaned against the wall outside Bill's hospital room. She didn't know how they were going to get past this.

She rested her head on the wall and looked up at the ceiling. "Lord, we need you now more than ever," she said. God's love and forgiveness were the only things that would help them get through this. She prayed for strength and healing for the kids. She prayed that they would be able to forgive their father and not let resentment into their hearts.

* * *

"WHERE IS MICHAEL?" Mary Elle asked as soon as she walked into the house and found Wyatt and Thomas in the living room. She had caught a ride with Tiffany and David from the hospital. They had dropped Melanie off at her house before heading here. Tiffany brought Ryder with them because Melanie still deserved to enjoy her wedding night even with everything that happened.

"He left. We tried to stop him, but he said he just wanted to be alone," Thomas said before pulling her into a hug.

The weight of the day fell over her. She wanted nothing more than to break down in the arms of the man that now held her heart. But she had to find Michael. She needed to see where his head was right now. She could sort through her thoughts and emotions later.

"Mom, you're shaking. Have a seat," Tiffany said.

"No, we need to find your brother. Where could he be?"

"Michael said he was going to the airport and would reach out when ready to talk. I think he's embarrassed and hurt," Thomas told her as he took her hand and guided her to sit in an armchair.

"I hate that this happened. Things were going well in our family. I thought Dad had changed. What he did for Mrs. Adelman meant so much to me," Tiffany said as she sat on the sectional sofa.

"Your dad has been working hard since the divorce to

change. We shouldn't let what Samantha did take away from that. Your father had no control over what she did. She acted on her own."

"How are you not upset?"

Mary Elle could hear the pain in Tiffany's voice, and she wished there was something she could do to take it away. Why did these things keep happening to their family? Why couldn't they just be happy?

"Forgiving your father might not change our past, but by forgiving him, we are not letting the past control our future. We can move forward with God's love in our hearts and have brighter days."

"I know you're right, mom. It just really sucks. David and I should get going. He has a long day at the sanctuary tomorrow, and I'll spend the day with my favorite little man," Tiffany said as she picked Ryder up and planted a few kisses on his head.

"I hope you're able to get some rest, Tiff. I love you. Your father might have made some mistakes in the past, but he loves you all so very much, too," Mary Elle said as she walked them out.

"I know, mom. I love him too, but it's just taking a little time to get back to normal."

"I understand, sweetheart. Goodnight," Mary Elle said as she kissed her goodnight.

Once they drove off, Mary Elle turned off the lights and headed upstairs to her, where Thomas was waiting for her.

"How are you feeling?" he asked with all the love in the world displayed in his eyes.

"Oh, Thomas," Mary Elle said as she crashed into his arms and finally let herself cry.

Thomas didn't say anything. He held her in his arms and stroked her back. Once she was done crying, he had her at arm's length and asked, "is there anything I can do for you?"

"No, I just want to sleep."

"I ran a warm bath for you while you were downstairs. It should be ready."

"Thank you. A bath would be nice," Mary Elle said as she lightly kissed him on the lips before heading to the bath.

CHAPTER 16

DeeAnn had been searching for her biological father, and now Paul was also helping in her search.

"Dee, you'll never believe it!" Paul said with so much emotion that DeeAnn got a bit nervous.

"What is it, Paul? Is everything ok?"

"Yes, I'm sorry if I frightened you. I found your father." Paul said as he rushed to DeeAnn's side and shook her softly.

"Really? Are you sure it's him?"

"I'm 99% certain, DeeAnn. He has a connection to Willow Heights. He is now living in Canton, here in Georgia." Paul said.

"I don't know what to say or do," DeeAnn said as tears ran down her face. She was happy to know Paul had found him but was also afraid to be rejected or that it would turn out not to be her father.

"We can call him before we visit," Paul said as he gave DeeAnn a paper with a phone number on it.

"I'm so nervous. What if he's not my father? What if he

doesn't know I exist? What if he doesn't want to know about me?"

"We'll never know unless you call and speak to him"

"You're right. I have nothing to lose and everything to gain."

"That's it! You can do this. Are you calling him today?"

"Yes, I'm just trying to figure out how to tell him who I am and explain everything."

"Sweetie, I'm here. We can both speak to him if this is the wrong number, no big deal. I'll keep looking. We won't stop looking until we find him. If it is him, we will speak to him and see if he's willing to meet you. I'll be there to support you every step of the way. You're not alone."

"Thank you. I appreciate all you've done and for finding this information. Let's call him right now."

DeeAnn took her cellphone out of her pocket, dialed the number, and put the call on speaker so both she and Paul could hear and talk to her father.

The phone rang once. No one answered. The phone rang a second time. No one picked up. DeeAnn felt a sinking feeling in her stomach when suddenly someone answered.

"Hello?" a man said.

"Hello, is this Mr. Greggory Bennett?" DeeAnn asked, hoping it was her father, the man she knew she needed to find, to bring closure to her many questions. Paul took her hand and squeezed it.

"Yes, that's me. Who is this?" he said.

DeeAnn looked over at Paul with an excited grin on her face. Paul was equally enthusiastic. They had done it! They found her father.

"I'm...my name is DeeAnn Sloane. I believe you knew my mother. Her name was Gladys Sloane."

"Gladys...yes, I knew her."

"Would I be able to visit with you...to talk about Gladys?"

"Of course. I would love to visit with her daughter. When can you visit?"

"I can visit this weekend if that's ok with you."

"I have my son visiting on Saturday, but I am free Sunday afternoon," Greggory said.

"That works for me. I'll be there Sunday." DeeAnn said excitedly.

"It was a delightful surprise receiving your call, DeeAnn," Greggory said as they hung up.

"Wow, I can't believe it! We found him, and now I'm meeting him," DeeAnn said as tears of joy filled her eyes.

"See, it all worked out. You were scared for no reason. Do you want me to go with you tomorrow?" Paul asked.

"Yes, you can come with me. I owe this to you. Thank you!" DeeAnn said as she wrapped her arms around Paul's neck and gave him a sweet kiss on the lips.

"How about we celebrate this occasion with some Chinese takeout?" Paul asked, knowing that DeeAnn loved Chinese food and was always up for it.

"I would love that. I'll have my usual," DeeAnn said as she went to the kitchen to grab the menu for Paul. He always wanted to try something new from their favorite Chinese restaurant. DeeAnn loved their honey chicken with fried rice and a wonton soup, usually shared with Paul.

"Let's see; I think I'll try the stir-fried vegetable with chicken and some dumplings," Paul said as he dialed the restaurant to place the order for delivery.

"I'll look for a movie to watch while we eat. What are you in the mood to watch?"

"Something funny. I need a good laugh. The kind that makes your belly ache."

"Oh, ok, let's see. I think I found the perfect movie. It's an oldie, but it's hilarious."

"When are you going to tell Mary Elle about your father?" Paul asked DeeAnn in a serious tone of voice.

"I was just thinking about that. I never keep things from her. At first, she wasn't too fond of me looking for my father because, to her, we are family no matter who our biological parents are, but she understood my reasons when I explained to her how I'd felt all these years. I guess I'll tell her when I see her tomorrow."

"I didn't mean to pressure you. It's in your timing, not mine."

"I know, but I honestly was thinking about when and how to tell her. I know she'll be happy for me."

"Ok, I know she will be happy for you. She's a very kind person. I admire her and Thomas adopting Wyatt."

"That was an amazing thing they did for him. He's a great kid too. He just needs direction and love."

* * *

BRITTNEY WAS WAITING for Jasper in the barn. She knew he had never had breakfast before work, so she'd stopped by the Busy Bee Coffee Shop to surprise him. After the wedding, she'd flown back to Kansas with her mother, and they spent a lot of time healing. They were now going to counseling with the church pastor together. Brittney was looking forward to fixing her relationship with her mother, but she knew she couldn't leave things with Jasper the way they had ended. He deserved to know the truth.

Brittney heard the door to the barn opening, and her heart started racing. She didn't know how Jasper would react when he saw her here.

"Hi Jasper," she said as he walked into the barn.

"Brittney, what are you doing here?"

"I want to clear things up with you. I don't like how we left things off."

"I'm listening…" he said and took a seat next to Brittney on a haystack.

Brittney turned to face him. She took a shaky breath before saying, "I like you, Jasper. I think you're great."

"But?"

"But there are some things in my life that no one knows about. Remember when you said it was easy for me to believe in love because I had a sheltered life with love all around me? Well, that couldn't be farther from the truth…" Brittney said as she began to tell Jasper about her upbringing. She told him how her father had abandoned them as soon as she was born. Her mother had fallen into a depression and was pretty absent from Brittney's life. They never had that mother-daughter bond that she had so desperately wanted from a young age. The only love Brittney felt growing up was from her grandmother.

"When my grandmother passed away, I spiraled. I felt alone in the world, and the only way I knew how to deal with it was to escape. I recreated my image and became an influencer. No one knew the real me, and no one ever cared to. As long as you look nice and tell a great story, no one cares about the rest."

"I care about the rest…" Jasper said quietly.

"I know you do, and that is why I came back. I value your friendship more than you can imagine. You let me be myself with you, and I never had to pretend. I love everything that I know about you, but I finally have a chance to form a relationship with my mom, and I want to focus on that for now."

"I don't need professions of love right now, Brittney. My love is patient. I'll be here whenever you're ready."

"I had a feeling you might say that. I've let my guard down with you, Jasper. It's something I never do. You crept inside my heart, and now I'm getting used to knowing what it's like to be accepted and loved for who I am."

"I was happy with the way my life was before you came along. I didn't think anything was missing. Now that I know you... I know that I want you in my life. I'll wait for you however long it takes."

"Thank you."

"How long are you staying here?"

"Just till Melanie returns from her honeymoon. I promised to help watch Ryder. She didn't want to over-whelm her mom."

"What are you doing Friday night?"

"Having dinner with you," Brittney said with a smile.

When she first came to Willow Heights, she came intending to help her best friend plan the wedding of her dreams. She didn't think that she would find herself and find someone who loved her for who she truly was in the process. Being here made her realize that life wasn't about the glitz and glamour and fame. Life was about family, love, and genuine friendships.

Brittney couldn't wait to fix her relationship with her mother. She knew it would take time to heal, but she was ready. Once she worked on herself, she would be prepared to enter a proper relationship with Jasper. He deserved to be with a woman that would love him and not hold back. He deserved the world, and Brittney would be that woman once she was ready.

EPILOGUE

"*E*veryone hide! He will be here any minute now!" Mary Elle said as she glanced at her watch.

In true Mary Elle fashion, she had planned a surprise birthday party for Thomas. He was turning 52 today, and she wanted him to know how much they all cared for and valued him. The whole gang was here, and Mary Elle couldn't think of a better way to show Thomas how they all cherished him. She told him that DeeAnn needed his help because the basement had flooded. He didn't suspect a thing, and that was the best part.

Mary Elle had prepared a dessert table with all kinds of delicious pastries and different chocolates. She'd driven to Atlanta, where there was a chocolatier that sold chocolates from all over the world. Thomas had a major sweet tooth, and chocolate was one thing he loved to indulge in.

"I think I hear a car!" DeeAnn said.

David took a peek from the living room window and said, "he's here!"

"I'm so nervous," Rita said with a giggle. She and Mary Elle were hiding in the kitchen.

Thomas knocked, and since no one answered a minute later, he stepped inside.

"Hello? Is anyone here?"

Tiffany had the cake ready and lit. She stepped out from where she'd been hiding near the stairs, and everyone began to sing happy birthday as they emerged from their hiding spots.

Thomas was all smiles, and when his eyes met Mary Elle's, he mouthed, "Thank you."

"I can't believe you're all here," Thomas said after blowing out his candles. He made his way around, greeting everyone and hugging them. When he reached Mary Elle, he wrapped his arms around her and squeezed her tight.

"Were you surprised?" she asked as she looked up at him.

"Yes, no one's ever thrown me a surprise party before."

"Really? I love surprise parties!"

Tiffany and David approached them, and they each took turns hugging and congratulating Thomas.

"Mary Elle, you did a great job," David said as he put an arm around her shoulders.

"Thanks. I am just glad everyone could make it. Did you see Vera, Thomas? She's somewhere around here."

"Yes, I was surprised to see her here. Thank you for doing this, sweetheart."

"We have some news to share with you guys," David said as he took Tiffany's hand.

"You're getting married?" Mary Elle asked a little too loudly. The whole room went quiet, and all eyes were on them.

"Sorry to disappoint, but no, not yet anyway," David said with a laugh.

Tiffany, standing next to him, was now completely red in the face. "The news is that David and I are running for the Towns Council."

"Elections are coming up, and we would like to replace Valerie and Richard."

"That's great news, you guys!" Thomas said.

"Yes, we need people that love our town, and that will fight for us," Mrs. Adelman said.

"Exactly, we saw how they treated you, and we should not stand for that. Our community is our top priority, and it's time that we got back to our roots. Willow Heights is about family and our values. It's time we start fighting for what's ours."

"You never stop making me proud, son," Thomas said as he hugged David again.

"Paul and I have some news to share," DeeAnn said.

"Oh! Are you getting married?" Mary Elle asked.

"Elle, stop trying to marry us all off!" DeeAnn said with a giggle.

"I'm sorry, I couldn't help myself!" Mary Elle said and pretended to zip her lips and throw the key away.

"We found my biological father, and we're going to meet him," DeeAnn said.

"Oh, Dee. I'm so happy for you!" Mary Elle said as she pulled her sister into a hug.

"How did you find him? Did he know about you?" Rita asked.

"I don't know yet. I didn't want to say anything over the phone. I just said I wanted to talk to him about my mother. He said he remembered her fondly and would love to meet to talk about her."

"That's fantastic, DeeAnn. I know how important it is to finally get answers to all the questions you might have in your mind," Sienna said.

DeeAnn had tears streaming down her face and couldn't find her voice to form a response. She nodded in agreement.

"Does anyone have any other good news to share?" Mary Elle asked as she glanced around the room.

"Jasper is going to Kansas for two weeks to meet my mom," Brittney said.

"She's going to love Jasper. I am so happy you have been able to make things right with your mom, Brittney."

Brittney moved to Kansas shortly after Melanie returned from her honeymoon. She moved in with her mother, and they worked on their relationship. Brittney seemed much happier now than she had ever been. Mary Elle remembered the first time she met Brittney when she visited Willow Acres; she had appeared happy, but her smile never truly met her eyes. She had always seemed to hold something back. Now that she had come clean about her past to her friends and millions of followers, she was finally free. Brittney had been afraid that her followers would lose interest, but many reached out and shared stories of their own. They thanked her for coming clean and said they found her easier to relate to now.

Mary Elle thanked God for Brittney's life and the life of all those in this room. Life wouldn't be as sweet as it was without these people here. They might face hard times, but they always got through them together. Life was hard and confusing sometimes, but it all worked out in the end. She thanked God for her ex-husband, Bill as well. He was a work in progress like the rest of them. Their relationships with him might not be back to normal yet, but Mary Elle knew that God would bring them all back together again in time.

* * *

THANK you for reading The Wedding at Willow Heights. I hope you enjoyed it! The next book in the series is Secrets in Willow Heights. Click here if you'd like to join DeeAnn as she explores her relationship with her father. Click here for Reconnecting in Willow Heights.

IF YOU WOULD LIKE to meet the characters of Winding Creek, click here. Your favorite characters from the Willow Heights series also make an appearance there.

LET'S BE FRIENDS!
Join Abigail's Newsletter for reminders of upcoming releases.

JOIN ABIGAIL'S Reader Group for: First Looks, exclusive giveaways, and more!

www.ingramcontent.com/pod-product-compliance
Lightning Source LLC
Chambersburg PA
CBHW050535160726